BACK TO THE WELL

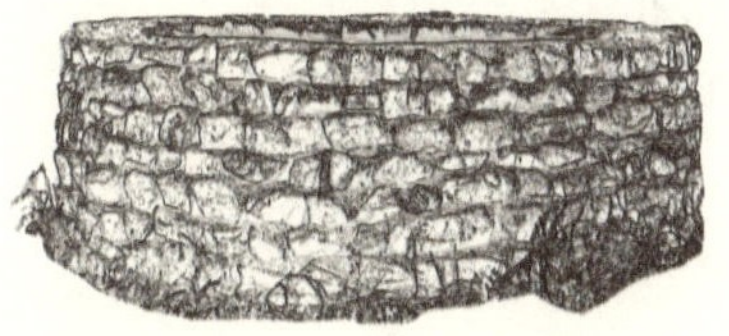

BACK TO THE WELL

AN ARGENTINIAN GHOST STORY

GUSTAVO BONDONI

GUARDBRIDGE BOOKS
ST ANDREWS, SCOTLAND

Published by Guardbridge Books,
St Andrews, Fife, United Kingdom.

http://guardbridgebooks.co.uk

Back to the Well.

Cover art by David Stokes
Well photo © Ilkin Guliyev | Dreamstime.com

ISBN: 978-1-911486-87-9

BACK TO THE WELL

DELFINA smiled into the wind. The hot air coming through the open window blew her hair back into the rear seat area. She didn't care. She'd been waiting her entire life for this.

She glanced over to where Joaco sat behind the steering wheel. He sensed her glance and grinned over at her.

"Told you," he said.

"You did," Delfina replied. "You were right. Look at this place."

"I know. I *know.*" He laughed gleefully as he slowed the car on the old two-lane highway and turned into the little town. In the distance, sand-colored mountains framed the vista perfectly, highlighting the lush trees at the base of the hills.

Joaco slowed, turned off the main highway, a dusty two-lane that wound its way through Western Argentina just a few miles from the border with Chile, and entered the town. White, single-story houses huddled around a dusty main street barely wide enough for two cars to pass side by side. A brown dog ran alongside the car for two blocks, barking madly into Delfina's open window before losing interest.

Joaco parked in front of a church, made of yellowish-grey stone that appeared to have been mined from the hills. It looked really old, like it had been built by the Spanish back during colonial times. They got out of the car. Delfina took a deep breath and coughed. They'd stirred up a large amount of dust.

Then she laughed at herself. "This is like standing next to an open oven door," she said. "Except with dust."

"Yeah. But look at that sky," Joaco said. "I don't even know what color to use to describe it. Cobalt? Turquoise?"

She smiled as he stared upwards. They'd met in class at the Universidad de Buenos Aires. He claimed to be a poet at heart, studying sociology because his parents—no-nonsense working class types who'd fought their entire lives to get ahead and have enough money to allow their only child to go to college—had insisted he needed something to pay the bills, and poetry wasn't going to cut it. Sociology might allow him a career with one of the political groups that worked with the country's poor. Strangely, he never showed much interest in politics: his mind was on women and poetry. He was constantly searching for the right words to express the numinous character of his thoughts.

"Bullshit," she said. "It's just blue."

He grinned at her. "That's because you're about as romantic as the paving stones." He kicked at the floor. "Hey, have you seen these paving stones? They're hexagons."

"Yeah, fascinating," Delfina said. "And don't forget dusty. Where do you think everyone is?"

"At home, having their siesta. This is Salta, not Buenos Aires. People still observe the old customs."

"So why did we stop?"

"I wanted to check out the little church," he replied, pointing behind him. "Have you ever seen such a cute thing?"

"Cute? Is that one of your fancy poet words?"

"Yeah, like the ones you like for me to call you in bed. You never seem to complain about those."

She grinned and blew him a kiss and danced along the dirt sidewalk to the stairs leading to the church. She stepped in front of the door, pulled out her phone and took a picture of the grey wood, bleached by the sun but still streaked with darker grey. Rusted nails, complete with bits of old paper stuck to them, emerged from deep inside the wood.

She popped the image onto her Instagram feed, generated a few hashtags and looked up.

Joaco rolled his eyes at her. "Are you quite done?"

"Hadn't uploaded yet, but that's probably just the cell connection here," she replied, popping the phone in her pocket and ignoring his impatience. He was the kind of guy who thought social media was stupid… which made him a complete Neanderthal, and also seemed a bit cute.

They pushed the door open to reveal a small nave, painted in white.

She crossed herself as she passed from the heat of the early afternoon sun into the cool interior of the holy building. No wonder many of the natives of little towns like this one had converted so thoroughly to Catholicism: all you had to do was step into a church in summer to realize that something magical had to be happening. Why were churches always so pleasant inside? Of course, it helped that the people who enjoyed this cool clammy interior were never exposed to real winters in drafty old churches. That would have changed some minds.

A smoke-darkened crucifix hung above the little altar at the far end. The church had no chapels in the wings—it was too small for that—but a couple of paintings hung on the walls: a nativity and what appeared to be an annunciation, in the old colonial style, that crude southern shadow of the Cuzco school. She quickly photographed them, but decided not to test Joaco's patience by posting them immediately.

"Good afternoon," a voice said. "Have you had a pleasant trip?"

Joaco said nothing, but Delfina rushed over. "Hello, father," she said. "We had a great trip. This place is beautiful."

The priest blinked and she realized one eye was completely white, blind. The other was dark blue. He appeared to be in his late thirties, blond and thin, with a short stubble. His black cassock had been washed almost grey.

He smiled. "I'm delighted to hear that. Are you up from Cordoba? Or Mendoza, Maybe?"

"Farther than that, father," she replied, standing on his left side so she wouldn't have to look into the blind, staring orb. "We're all the way up from Buenos Aires."

"That's quite a drive," he replied. "Fifteen hundred kilometers."

"We're on vacation," Delfina said.

"Ah, yes. The winter vacation. You are in school?"

"University."

"Of course."

"And you?" The man didn't sound like he was from Argentina, not even from northwestern Argentina, where they spoke more like Chileans than like Argentines.

The priest smiled sadly. "I'm from Bolivia. I was the only man the Archdiocese could get who actually preferred to officiate in a tiny place like this. I came of my own free will, would you believe it?"

"Do you get many people in mass?"

"I have my flock. It's probably not the kind you're used to in the great cities, but there is work for the lord to do here as well." He turned his head so the blind eye was closer to her. His gaze fell to the golden cross on her neck. "You're a believer. What church do you attend?"

"I... I haven't been to church in three years."

He smiled gently. "That wasn't my question."

"I used to attend the Iglesia Santa Rita in San Isidro," she said. "It's a small church."

"Small, but influential," the priest said.

"I suppose," she replied. She wasn't surprised that this man knew of Santa Rita. Everyone always knew about Santa Rita, no matter where she went in the country. "My family has been going there for two hundred years."

He nodded knowingly. "And I imagine you have several priests to your family's name. Perhaps a bishop or two?"

"I guess," she replied. "I have an uncle who is a priest."

The priest smiled. "Are you planning on staying long?"

"At least the night," she replied. "It's a beautiful town."

"More than that," Joaco said. "I already feel this town inspiring me. Is there a hotel?"

The priest looked at Joaco as if he were seeing him for the first time. "There is. Out beside the highway. But a couple like you won't like it. It's designed for traveling salesmen and their… occasional companions. I recommend staying with Doña Julia. She has rooms to rent out to the occasional foreign tourist we get. But I'm sure she'll give a couple of Argentine kids a good local price."

"That's good. We're on a budget," Joaco replied.

It was true. He'd insisted on paying for everything, from the meager savings he'd accumulated after doing some shifts at a Starbucks. Fortunately, he lived with his parents, so he saved most of what he earned.

It was a good thing he'd offered to pay. Her parents would never have loaned her money for a trip like this. She'd had to tell them she was going with two female friends… girls from university who'd been only too happy to lie for her. Or, more precisely, they'd been delighted to, as they said, 'help her escape from the oppression of her religio-patriarchal parents.'

Either way, she'd convinced her parents that everything was on the level, and had been posting perfectly innocent things onto her Instagram account since. Her mom spent most of her days on her phone, and the pictures of churches and mountains were what she wanted to see. So Delfina made sure that was what she saw.

She snapped a photo of the priest in his church, and asked him his name for the caption.

"Padre Hermindez," the man replied.

They thanked him and walked to the house he'd indicated, a slightly larger compound than others in the town, hidden behind a wall. A dun-colored wall.

No doorbell—at least no visible doorbell—adorned the tall gate, so they tried the handle. Half the door opened outward to reveal a lush green garden.

"Wow," Delfina said, "where do they get all the water for this?"

"From the river, most likely."

"What river?"

"The road crossed a bridge over it as we entered the village from the highway. Didn't you look?"

She thought about it, then shook her head. "I didn't. I guess I was looking at the mountains."

He nodded. "I can understand that. I might have missed it if I hadn't been driving."

"So why is the rest of the town dusty and desert-like?"

"I guess it must be the wind and the heat. This garden is inside a wall and irrigated, or it wouldn't be here. But you can tell there's lots of water around because there are plenty of trees on those hills."

A path led away from the water-stained walls, through the lush vegetation led to a squat yellow house surrounded on all sides by a roofed porch. It was the only wooden structure they'd seen since they entered the town. Half-seen creatures—*mice?* Delfina wondered—skittered away as they climbed the single step that led to the porch and knocked on the pink door.

The woman who opened the door had dark skin, dark eyes and hair that had once been black as night, but was now streaked with grey. She peered at them and said: "Five thousand pesos a night. Because you're Argentine."

Juaco looked like he was about to argue. Then he seemed to remember just how cheap that actually was, and deflated. "Can we see the room?"

The woman held his gaze. "Yes. But there's no need. You'll like it."

"How do you know?"

"Because it has a bed," the woman replied. "And you two are in love. Or something like love."

Something like love, Delfina thought, was the perfect description of what they had. She didn't think it was love. There was fun. And excitement. And yes, there was a lot of physical attraction: Joaco was a good-looking guy, in a disheveled, ten-day-beard sort of way. And the fact that he was so different from all the boys she'd grown up with and gone to school with made it feel a little dangerous, a little forbidden, every time he took her to bed. And he was a poet, which was somehow both a little lame and incredibly cool at the same time. But not love. *Something* like love.

The first thing she noticed about the room was that the floor was made of grey wood that looked like it would feel dry to her feet. No rich, thick varnishes.

The bed was frilly and feminine, with pillows, in pastel pinks, pale greens and light blues. Several potted plants sat in a stand beside one wall. The window had slatted shutters which allowed daylight to filter in at an angle, and there was a desk, complete with wicker chair—with flowered cushions of course—beside it. The tropical furnishings were all wrong for an Argentine colonial house, but perfect for the heat of the day.

"You were right," she said with a smile. "We like it."

"And I suppose you'll be wanting the bed right away."

"I could use some rest," Joaco replied. "It's been a long drive."

The woman nodded knowingly, closed the door and left them alone.

"She seems nice," Delfina said.

"She owns a hotel. I guess most young couples don't have a lot of depth to them when they reach a hotel."

"And you say I'm not romantic," she said. "Look around. Have you ever been in a more romantic room? It's like being on the set of an old Hollywood movie set in Cuba or something."

"Back when Cuba was exploited, you mean."

"I suppose," Delfina replied. "But also when Cuba was romantic." Again, she remembered too late that it was better to leave certain subjects alone when Joaco was around. He hated that certain Argentines chose to travel abroad, to spend money the country needed to fatten foreign coffers. Likewise the concept that one's patrimony was one's to spend as one chose—and not something that should be at the disposal of the state—was alien to him.

He looked around dubiously. "You really like this room?"

"A lot more than I like the motels with red lights and porn videos you usually choose."

"Then ask for it."

She almost refused, almost asked him to respect her. But what fun would that be. This wasn't a guy she wanted to marry. He was a guy to have some fun with. She'd grab a good-looking engineer or company manager when the time came, and they'd have a lot more in common than she did with Joaco. So she simply undid the clasp of her jeans and let them drop to the floor, along with her panties.

"Fuck me," she said.

"Yeah, that's what I like. A high-class whore begging for it."

"I'm not begging," Delfina replied. "I'm ordering you. Now, are you going to do it or am I going to have to find some other poor boy?"

Even in the dim yellow light of the ancient incandescent bulb, she saw his pupils dilate with every word, and he came at her like a bull.

"Yes, princess."

* * *

She woke from her nap to find him already awake, sitting at the desk with a cigarette hanging from his mouth, unlit. He was wearing only the same boxer shorts she'd torn off a little earlier and was bent over a sheet of paper on the desk. It was one of his special poetry sheets: unlined, yellowish paper that he said was a creamy experience.

Those were his words: creamy experience. It sounded, like every time he tried to turn something everyday into poetry, slightly dirty. Or maybe she just associated him with a slightly dirty feeling in herself, the way she was knowingly rebelling against everything her family thought she should be doing.

On this paper of creamy experience, he was writing with the most common ballpoint pen imaginable: a blue Bic with the hard plastic cracked and chipped at the back.

"Inspiration struck in the middle of our nap?" she asked.

He looked over at her. "Are you a fairy princess, to appear unannounced in the semi-darkness?"

"I don't know," she replied. "You called me some

very different things before. I suppose it's a question of mood."

"You speak in riddles," he said. "But these are riddles that I need to capture on paper."

"Yeah, whatever. I'm going to take a shower."

The nearest bathroom—Doña Julia had shown them three separate ones, shared among the guests—stood across the hall from their room, so she dressed, grabbed some clean underwear from the soft bag she'd packed, and headed over.

The water was perfect—hot enough and with plenty of pressure, but also much sweeter than the water she normally used in Buenos Aires. It probably came straight from a well, or maybe the river, and didn't have the chlorinated taste that water did in the capital. Of course, it was probably not quite as free of microbes, but what did that matter? It wasn't like the province of Salta was in the middle of a cholera epidemic. She let the water pour around her mouth.

After a shower so long that it that would probably call up Doña Julia's ire, she scrubbed herself dry with the tiny hand towel in the bathroom. It never occurred to her that a hotel might not have plenty of fresh towels just waiting to be used… but this wasn't a hotel. She supposed it made sense that you had to bring your own when sharing a bathroom with other guests.

Except she hadn't seen any other guests.

She dressed and was about to cross back into their room but, on a whim, she walked down the hall. Doña Julia had said there was a covered patio that opened up onto the garden, and that there was a communal kitchen, so she walked down the hall.

It was quite short. Three more doors opened to the

exterior of the house before the hall turned left and the outer side of the hallway turned into a room full of recliners and little tables. Vines grew in a concrete structure overhead. The air that came from the garden was much more tropical than she'd come to expect over the past day or two of driving through western Argentina: to the ubiquitous heat was added humidity she could feel on her skin. It got between the hairs of her forearms, and she rubbed them absently.

It was hard to imagine that just a little further west you could ski on the slopes of the Andes, and that in Buenos Aires they'd been freezing their butts off. Now, it seemed they'd arrived in an endless summer that, combined with the way their room looked like something out of 1940s Key West, made her feel time didn't apply here.

The vegetation extended to the walls that surrounded the compound but, because you could barely see the boundaries from the little room, it made the gardens feel enormous.

It reminded her of a hotel she'd once gone to in the Amazon jungle, where her parents had expected to spend a week learning about living in peace with nature… but where she and her brothers had spent the week in the swimming pool.

Delfina walked around the house to return instead of going through the hall. The little roofed porch actually ran all the way around the house, which meant that she could walk straight past the exterior windows. They were all shuttered, but from one of them—two windows down from the one to their room—came the soft sound of weeping.

She stopped at the one she thought was theirs, and

peeked between the slats. Fortunately, she could only see as the desk and part of one wall, so no one would have been able to watch them making love. She saw Joaco scribbling furiously.

Smiling impishly, she knocked on the window.

It opened and Joaco blinked against the afternoon light. "Ah, the fairy princess," he said. "You look much better in the garden than you did in the bed."

"You want to come for a walk? Maybe get something to eat?"

He looked at her as if he didn't understand what she was saying then shook his head. "A fairy princess shouldn't need to eat." Then he began to compose. She saw the words 'fairy princess' on the page. "I'm inspired now."

Delfina stared at him for a few moments, trying to let him know, without words, that he was acting weird in a way she didn't find cute, but he only looked up once, and stared at the mountains.

"Whatever," she said after a while and, pausing only long enough to toss her used underwear into the room, she walked away. She was glad she'd taken a roll of bills and her phone into the bathroom earlier, or she would have had to go around to get them—either that or climbed in through the open window.

Doña Julia was nowhere to be seen, so Delfina let herself out through the main gate and walked up the street. She googled how long the siesta hour lasted in Salta, but the page failed to load, so tried to remember what she knew about siestas in the interior of the country. She thought she remembered that it could last until five PM, so maybe she'd see some people out and about soon enough.

For now, however, the streets belonged to her. The dusty hexagons of the paving stones seemed to reflect the heat of the day back up at her, but it was a dry heat: all the humidity was locked up in Doña Julia's garden.

Delfina walked past the church. Not even the cool interior would convince her to go inside now that she had the pictures she needed to mollify her mother. She would return on Sunday, if they were still in town. Joaco seemed to have been hit pretty hard by the place, and it was Friday, so she might be there for Sunday morning mass.

It was strange to think that, far from her family, she yearned to commune with the god she thought she'd left behind. Like how she'd spent her entire semester while on student exchange in Spain listening to Argentine rock she'd never paid all that much attention too when she lived in Buenos Aires.

But what else was there to do in this tiny place? She'd promised to let Joaco write his poetry if inspiration hit... but what could she do in the meantime? It seemed a little bitchy to complain about something she'd specifically promised.

She smirked. Florencia, a friend of hers, had been invited to a ski resort by her boyfriend... but since she didn't ski, she'd filled her hours by having sex with a guy she met. The woman had basically become the most popular girl in their circle of friends as she told the story over and over again. They all criticized her behind her back... but they were all jealous as hell.

Still, Joaco already made her feel like she was eating the forbidden fruit. Did she really want to go any further than that?

Delfina wasn't sure, but suspected she didn't. Even

before she'd gotten into the car with Joaco, she had decided to end it when they got back. He was different, and fun, and sexy enough… but she could only run on that sense of rebellion for so long. She was starting to get that empty feeling her friends talked about, that she'd never understood before. If a guy was fun and sexy, she thought she should feel happy, right? Did he also need him to be Mister Right?

She sighed. Apparently, she did.

Ugh.

Delfina kicked herself mentally. She shouldn't spend the entire vacation moping about what the vacation wasn't. She should spend it celebrating what it was. And what it was a chance to walk around a tiny little village on the western edge of Argentina, a place she didn't even imagine existed just a day before, up in the beautiful mountains just before the Andes got serious. People here had to live very differently from people in the city. They had to have a sense of peace that she, with her six hours of classes and four hours of unpaid internship at the Labor Ministry every day plus all the commuting could never imagine. How did these people fill up their time?

She bet they had deep thoughts in the big silences of the mountain.

A handwritten cardboard sign outside a whitewashed rectangular building said *Empanadas*, and she realized she hadn't eaten since a quick lunch at gas station restaurant two hours before turning into the tiny flyspeck of a town.

The woman inside told her that the local hand pies—meat or ham and cheese versions only, since veganism hadn't reached these parts except as just another funny story, only half-believed, about the weird behaviors the capital-dwellers engaged in—had been handmade just that morning. Delfina couldn't tell… they looked the same as every other empanada she'd ever eaten. She bought a half-dozen. Three of each flavor.

The woman who sold her the food could have been Doña Julia's older sister. Her skin was a little darker, her back a little more stooped, her hair a little grayer.

"Are you staying long?" the woman asked.

"Just a few days," Delfina replied.

"That's longer than most people stay," the woman said.

"It's a beautiful little town," Delfina replied.

"Carrizo is an old town," the woman said. "And we're old people."

Delfina had heard of the problem. One of her friends had done missionary work in the interior of the country, and had told them that one of the problems was that the half-abandoned towns were full of old people that no one took care of, because the younger generations had all migrated towards the cities. "The priest told me he gets people in his masses on Sunday. Families from up in the hills, I suppose."

The woman peered out onto the street, as if seeing it for the first time. "They're old people, too. Old souls that have been around here since the beginning. They've seen the wars and the conquest and were even here when the Spanish loyalists resisted the independentists right here in the town. It's the same people, over and over again."

"What tribe are you from?" Delfina asked. She regretted it even as she spoke the words. Many people—most people—were content to be Argentine. They didn't care what their ancestors were any more than the people from Buenos Aires cared whether their ancestors were Italian or Spanish or German or Polish. By now, Argentines were Argentines.

The woman shrugged. "I've never known. My family didn't have a tribe. They just lived on this land, in a community, far from anyone who could tell us who we were supposed to be."

"I thought because you were talking about reincarnation..."

"I don't know about that, either," the woman said with a sad smile. "I just told you what my grandmother said. I used to think the old lady was crazy. I'm sure you think I'm crazy. But as the years went by, I think she isn't as crazy as all that."

"I'm sure she was a very wise lady."

The other woman laughed. "You're a well-bred one, aren't you? Remind me of Jacinta. She ran the town when I was younger, but she's been dead for a long time. Well-bred and quiet, and would lie to anyone if she thought the truth would make them feel bad. My grandmother was not wise... and she certainly wasn't a lady. If she had been, my mother would have known her father."

Delfina walked away, leaving the woman chuckling to herself.

Within half an hour, she'd circumnavigated the entire town once, and was about to head into the center, which she hadn't yet explored. The town was... just a little town. Nothing special except for the fact that she hadn't run into anyone on her perambulations: these people really took their siesta seriously.

Despite the heat, she wasn't sweating—the sweat must have evaporated as soon as it formed—but she was thirsty. A *kiosko*, a small hole-in-the-wall candy store, had a large awning with the Coca-Cola logo on it. She asked for mineral water.

The kiosko's proprietor was a young man in his twenties—which meant the old woman might be a little bit crazy after all—who had the dark hair and skin of the other inhabitants of the town but also green eyes that looked like the eyes of a cat. He was trim, but the muscles of his arm and back showed through his shirt as he stretched to grab the water.

If I wanted to do what Florencia did, this is the guy I'd choose, she thought. *Right there on the floor of the back room while Joaco ignores me to write his awful poetry.*

The man smiled at her. "What do you think of Carrizo?" he asked.

Carrizo. The old woman had said the name as well.

"It's beautiful," she replied, completely honestly. "I don't know why more people don't come here." She looked around the kiosco. "And I don't know why everyone young has run for the capital. Isn't it better to live here?"

"Of course it's better here. But the mountains are best of all," the man replied with a ghost of a wistful smile. "If I could, I'd spend my life lost in the hills." He looked around the kiosco and the street outside. "But that's impossible, of course. A man must keep himself alive."

"I can only imagine how beautiful it must be if you know the trails."

"It's not about beauty. It's about quieting the voices."

He cocked his head at her. "You don't hear them, do you? I'm not surprised. You look like you come from a big city. There must be so many voices there that you learn to ignore them when you're a baby. But I don't. I hear them here, inside my head, every day of my life, and I wish I could be in the hills where the voices might be quiet."

Delfina forced out a smile, paid for her water and rushed away. At least she knew why this particular young man hadn't gone off to the city to make his future.

But, though the sun was still up in the sky and the little town was just as picturesque as it had been a few minutes before, her peace was shattered. She looked behind to see if the guy from the kiosko was following her all the way back to Doña Julia's place.

There was no sign of him. There was no sign of anyone. Even the dog they'd seen when they first drove into the town had probably decided to get inside and nap.

Joaco was still seated at the desk, still scribbling away as she entered. A neatly-stacked pile of yellowish paper stood on the desk beside him.

He looked up when she entered and rubbed his eyes. "Delfina? Have you been gone long?"

"Long enough to let you get it out of your system," she said. "I hope. Did it work?"

"I… I think so," he replied. He looked at the cream-colored stack as if he'd never seen it before. "I've never felt this urge to write so strong. Like the words were pouring into me."

"About fairy princesses?" she said, reaching over to pick up a sheet.

"Some of it was, yes."

Joaco made no move to stop her, so she read the poem at the top of the pile. She didn't know if it was the newest or the oldest. It had no title.

> *The dark holds the memories of what happened.*
> *The memories make the darkness forever.*
> *They wait for vessels to carry them out.*
> *Whispering their revenge for all to hear.*

She shook her head. It didn't seem very good to her. And it certainly wasn't the kind of romantic beauty she'd expected. Where were the roses in the hair of the ethereal fairy princess? Half the reason one screwed a poet was so that you could, five years down the line, buy a slim tome of his verse and say: "There. That's me. The languid Tinkerbell with limpid eyes."

"I brought empanadas," she said instead.

His eyes came alive. "Oh, God, I could eat a dozen of them."

"Well, I brought you three. Maybe three-and-a-half if I'm not too hungry."

"I'll take it," he replied. He smiled. "I'm really sorry. I don't know what came over me."

"Don't worry about it. I went for a walk," she said.

"Did you enjoy it?"

"I did… until I bought that water." She told him about the guy in the *kiosco*.

"Did he feel threatening?"

"No… not really. But the whole thing bugged me. For a second it felt like I was in a place I didn't belong. Like the beautiful town and the bright light were keeping me from seeing what's all around us."

"We're in a bedroom," Joaco said, looking around. "It

has wood-paneled walls which must have cost a fortune to put in." Then he held her eyes. "But more importantly, we're alone. Together."

He let his eyes scan downwards from her face, hungrily.

"Can we leave this place?" she said.

"Now? It will be dark in an hour or so. Where would we stay?"

Yes, she wanted to say. *Right now.*

But that would have been silly. It would also have been dangerous. The roads were scenic and beautiful, but the same winding desolation that made them beautiful also made them risky. The two-lanes that wound through the Andes foothills weren't built with night travel in mind.

"No, of course not. Tomorrow is fine. Besides, we already paid for the room," she said.

He nodded and they ate their empanadas. Though Delfina was so hungry she could have eaten a horse, she still saved him half of her final empanada. He thanked her, but she hadn't done it for him: she thought that, maybe, if he was happy, he would protect her.

"I should shower," he said.

"Ask Doña Julia for a towel," she said.

He nodded and headed out.

The late afternoon light had turned orange, but disappeared almost immediately as the mountains cast their shadows over everything. The wooden panels seemed to absorb the yellow light of the room.

She leaned back against the pillows, planning to wait for Joaco to return, but the long day, along with the fact that she'd just eaten, caused her to drift off.

* * *

She saw a circle of light up above. She was in a circular hole and couldn't climb out. The walls of the hole were paneled with wood, in a familiar square pattern. Something dark seeped through the cracks between two panels. She touched it, and her fingers came away dark red. The red of a deep, bubbling wound.

Blood pooled around her ankles. Her knees. Her chest. She tried to swim in the dark liquid, but instead of buoying her up, the blood pulled her into its depths. She thrashed violently and tried to climb the wooden walls.

Her hands slipped, leaving long bloody stripes on the elegant, square-patterned panels.

She went under and tried to swim.

Her head broke the surface. Then she sank again.

She tried to scream, but blood, thick and viscous and molasses-like, poured into her mouth and silenced her.

* * *

Delfina woke to see Joaco returning to the room. He held his clothes in a bundle against his chest. A white towel was wrapped around his waist and, as he pushed the door shut with his foot, he winked at her and let the towel drop.

She welcomed him into bed, not so much because she wanted him as because she wanted someone, anyone, to hold her.

* * *

Light through the open window woke her, and she reached out to find Joaco.

He wasn't there, so she opened an eye and looked around. He was sitting at the desk, staring slack-jawed at the paper in front of him, pen in hand.

"Joaco," she said. "Are you all right?"

He looked so much like dead people in movies, people that had died in place and looked alive until someone tried to move them and they keeled over, that she jumped out of bed, heedless of the open window and her nakedness, and pushed his shoulder.

He didn't topple from the chair to lie lifeless on the floor, but he didn't react in much of any other way, either.

"Joaco, I'm talking to you," she said.

He blinked, but she had no way of knowing whether it was in response to anything she'd said or simply because humans blinked every so often.

"Listen, let's get the hell out of here. I know you've been inspired here," she refrained from saying that he'd been inspired to write godawful poetry and the dribble on the sheet he was currently using didn't look much better, "but I don't like this place. We can stop on the next town over if you like. Same kind of people, exactly the same mountains."

He mumbled something. She thought she heard the words 'fairy princess', but she couldn't quite be certain. What was definite was that she was getting angry.

"Look," she said. "I'm going to get some breakfast. When I come back, you'd better be over this fucking artist's trance you're putting on. I know you think you're supposed to be some kind of deep poet, but you're just being an asshole."

The pen moved mechanically to the sheet, and more near-illegible scribbles flowed onto to the page.

Delfina cursed and left. She walked down the street, enjoying the breeze—still soft in the early morning, but with the promise of another extra hot day to come—and found a bakery. She bought a dozen and a half *facturas*, sweet croissant-like pastries, and headed back to Doña Julia's place.

There, she set the pastries on one of the tables in the patio and moved to the tiny kitchen to find a kettle. The place didn't have an electric kettle, so she turned on the gas stove and boiled water. Then she checked her phone.

It was blank. Dead. The battery must have zeroed out, and she tried to remember the last time she'd charged it. It must have been two days ago.

It was natural that it would slip her mind. She had barely used it since she arrived. A couple of pics of the church, a couple of google searches that never loaded because the cell coverage was crap. Other than that… nothing.

But she really, really wanted to talk to Jimena right now. Jimena was her best friend and confidant. She lived in New York now, but that didn't matter. What time was it in New York?

Too early. And besides, her charger was in the room. With Joaco. And she really wasn't in the mood to face him just yet. She'd give him a minute.

When the water boiled, she found two mugs, tossed a tea bag into each, and poured the water over them. Joaco liked maté with his breakfast, but screw him. She knew he'd drink tea in a pinch and didn't feel like coddling him right now.

Then she took a deep breath and headed back for their room. She found him exactly as she'd left him, bent over his poetry.

"I bought breakfast. I'm having it in the terrace

room There are *facturas*. Come if you like, but if you're not there in five minutes I won't wait."

Pausing only to grab her charger, she closed the door and stood in the hallway for a moment, counting to ten.

At the count of nine, soft sobs from the room two doors over reached her, and she hurried back to the patio. She moved her things so she could charge her phone in an outlet just beside the sliding doors that separated the exterior space from the interior of the hotel.

When she straightened, a person stood beside the window, just inside the slightly open panel. She gasped.

"I'm sorry. I didn't mean to frighten you," Doña Julia said. "Have you found everything to your liking?"

"Yes…" Delfina said.

"There's something wrong."

She didn't want to speak to this woman. She just wanted to leave this little flyspeck of a town forever and forget it existed. But the woman looked sternly down at her, expecting to hear some tale of cockroaches in the bedroom or another equally awful criticism of her housekeeping. "It's not the room. The room is lovely."

"But something's wrong."

"It's Joaco. He's acting strange."

"The young man you came with." The woman shook her head. "You're too good for the likes of him. Even a woman who's spent her entire existence in this town, and who never had any aspirations to gentility or culture can tell. You are from a different world, a world he will never be a part of."

Her first instinct was to defend Joaco, but something in the woman's tone made her hesitate.

Doña Julia didn't seem to be criticizing him. Or at least she wasn't doing so with malice. She just seemed to be stating a natural truth which was obvious to everyone. Just a little piece of conversation. Perhaps she just wanted Delfina to explain it was nothing serious, that it was just some meaningless sex, an expression of her freedom from social expectations.

Or perhaps Doña Julia already knew that. As the only person with rooms to rent in the entire town, she probably saw more than her fair share of couples and knew every possible way a man and a woman could relate to each other. When you compounded that over the number of years she was likely to have been doing this…

"I don't care about that. Social position isn't important. It's almost like he's… I don't know… possessed or something."

Doña Julia snorted, an absolutely unexpected sound. "People do not become possessed in this town. Or in this century. Padre Hermindez does what he can. No evil invades the minds of our people, no matter what spirits might roam the mountains." She gazed deep into Delfina's eyes. "Or of our visitors. Perhaps he's sensitive to the beauty of our place. Is he some kind of artist?"

"A poet." Then she grinned evilly. It was nice to have someone she could be bitchy with, someone who didn't matter. "But I definitely wouldn't call him an artist."

The old woman smiled, an expression of tolerance for the slight she knew Delfina intended. "It's how he sees himself, how his mind functions that matters. Particular beauty can cause strange reactions."

"Well, I don't care. Once I finish these *facturas*, I'm going to have a look at the display in the town hall. I saw a sign for it yesterday. And if he isn't here, I'm not going to wait for him."

But when Doña Julia walked away, Delfina shed a single tear of loneliness and frustration.

Then she ate ten of the pastries, an amount that would keep her going all day.

* * *

Though she'd never been in the town hall of a little place like this before in her life—not that she could recall at least, though her parents might have taken her as a kid, when she was too small to resist—Delfina was convinced it must be exactly the same as all the other town halls of forgotten provincial communities everywhere. It took its place in history a lot more seriously than anyone else ever would.

So she spent two hours reading every word of the little signs that told the story of the history of the region in 1810, the year of Argentine independence from Spain.

At first, she read to eat up a big chunk of time, to put off as long as possible the inevitable nightmare that awaited when she got back to the hotel room.

But after a few lines, she was fascinated in spite of herself. The drama that had played out among the subtropical mountains in the region might have been irrelevant in the larger scheme of things… but it must have been thrilling to the men and women involved.

When tidings of the Declaration of Independence reached the town—the city in which the declaration was signed, Tucuman, was just a couple of day's ride distant, even in that era of dusty trails and slow coaches—the town immediately split into two factions.

Spanish loyalists were composed of an extended family of cattle-owners along with people who'd received land grants from the crown, and they were afraid that their enemies among the revolutionaries would think to annul the privileges. They made up the wealthier people in town and represented about forty of the four hundred and fifty townsfolk.

Everyone else stood against them, firmly in the revolutionary camp. That this was mainly for fiscal reasons was not stated in the official documents, but it could be easily be inferred by the fact that the current landowners were on one side of the revolution and the people who worked for them were on the other.

Still, what happened next was interesting.

The loyalists hired a small band of mercenaries to force the townsfolk to declare the town against the Revolution.

The townsfolk initially fled into the hills but, at night, using their greater knowledge of the area, they attacked the mercenary camp and killed every last man of them. Then, when day arrived, they rounded up the loyalists and held them in a heavily-guarded tent city while they awaited word from Tucuman about what to do next.

On the third day, the loyalists attempted to escape during the night, but a lookout, a small boy of six years of age, spotted them.

Caught mid-flight, the loyalists took refuge in the church—the very church that Delfina and Joaco had visited. At length, the townsfolk managed to bash the doors down and opened fire into the church.

By dawn, the loyalists were dead.

Fearing disease, the townsfolk lugged the loyalists

to a dry well, dropped them inside, and covered the well with stones.

Each of these events were arrayed on display cases that lined the walls, with hand-drawn diagrams, maps and portraits illustrating the proceedings. The final case was filled with photographs showing the September 17th celebrations—that was the date of the events—and displayed a certificate that awarded this little backwater the distinction of being a Hero Town of the Revolution.

It was all extremely Third-worldy.

Delfina sighed. Not because, now that she'd read the story, the town hall lost most of its appeal, becoming just another dreary public building, but also because the confrontation with Joaco would have to happen soon. It was around lunchtime, but there was no way she could eat. The *medialunas* still rumbled in her stomach.

"Dammit," she said. Then she walked down the worn red tiles of the town hall and out onto the baking street. She walked with all the enthusiasm of a condemned prisoner, trying to find an excuse, any excuse to put it off.

But the houses, whitewashed with yellow accents, gave her no such excuse. They just stood there, absorbing the sun.

The magical garden, so cool and moist, broke the trance. As she entered Doña Julia's compound, she collected her thoughts and headed to their room.

Joaco was exactly where she'd left him that morning. "I brought some food," she said, hoping the fight wasn't forthcoming.

He didn't even look up from his page.

"Are you going to sit there forever?" she said. "Are you going to ignore me?"

Three furious steps brought her to his side and, without thinking, she swatted the pen in his hand. It bounced on the table and flew out the window, to disappear into the bushes outside.

"Oh, fuck. I'm sorry," she said. "I'll find it."

Halfway to the door, she stopped. Other than sitting up straight in his chair and blinking a couple of times, Joaco hadn't acknowledged her return, or even the violence done to his pen.

"Are you all right?" she asked.

"Yes, I'm fine," he replied.

With that response, her concern was crushed under the weight of her fury. "Then why the hell haven't you spoken to me in two days?"

"The poetry. It's singing in my head." He smiled. "I've never felt this way before."

"Well, are you going to come do something with me?"

He shook his head gently. "No. I can't stop now. Maybe later."

"There won't be a later, Joaco. Either you get out of that chair right the fuck now, or I'm walking out of your life."

He took a long time to answer. Finally, he replied: "I'm sorry." His hand fumbled as if searching for something, but his pen was nowhere to be found.

Delfina didn't even wait to see if he was bluffing. She just threw her clothes into her bag—a soft green one with a shoulder strap—and left the room, slamming the door behind her.

He probably couldn't pay for the room. So what? Fuck him.

Then she went to the town center and found a bar with wooden tables and chairs. She ordered a *milanesa* with French fries and forced it down. She wasn't hungry, but she didn't know when she would eat again if she managed to get on some kind of bus…

She signaled the waiter, a man with the kind of mustache one only saw on elderly waiters anymore, to come to her table.

"Is everything all right, miss?" the man asked.

"Yes, the food is fine," she replied. "I was wondering if there's a bus service…" she almost asked if there was a bus service to civilization, to anywhere with a decent cell connection, but caught herself in time. "…to Salta."

"Oh, yes," the man said. "There's an evening bus that goes all along the mountain towns and ends in Salta around midnight. You can catch it at the stop on the traffic circle just before the bridge at seven."

She knew exactly where that was. She'd noticed it when they drove into town. "Thank you," she said.

Her watch told her it was almost two-thirty. She'd dawdled over lunch as much as she could, but she couldn't return to the hotel room. Not for anything in the world.

So she walked the baking streets, still deserted, as they always seemed to be during the hours she was out and about, until she came to a playground. Well, it was a playground if you could call a set of swings in the center of a packed-dust square a playground. She sat in the shade of a tree.

Within moments, she felt sleepy and, placing her bag under her head, closed her eyes for a moment.

* * *

The green grass got its emerald color from the blood of the thousands of men who'd died there. The battleground could have been anywhere: north of Córdoba, on the arid plains near Ceuta, on the lush pampas and altiplanos of South America. Blood had watered all of them, and they all melted into one, the grass she stood on.

Delfina wanted to get the hell out of there. She felt death all around her, not as something imminent, but as wisps of memory. Here, a tendril of blinding pain as a sword slid between two plates of armor and into an armpit. There, the scream of a pageboy as the hooves of a war horse crushed his skull. Further, like the remembrance of smoke, the lingering ache of infection as it took a young musketeer's life.

Alongside the impressions of death rose mist, a grey-blue fog that concealed Delfina's feet and legs as far as her knees.

From the fog emerged figures. A bearded knight in a medieval helmet. A prehistoric villager in rags clutching a spear with a stone head. An eighteenth-century rifleman in Napoleonic dress of some sort. A man in a white button-down shirt and a red bandanna. Countless more, stretching back in time.

She knew without being told that every man looking at her had died in battle. Perhaps a noble death in a heroic charge. More likely of a weapon he never saw coming, while fighting to control his bladder and put down the terror he felt. A terror that, in every case, was justified.

They stepped towards her, and Delfina wanted to run, but the mist around her knees held her tight. She couldn't even step backward to avoid the figures.

A hand reached out for her. A thousand. Outstretched, pleading, desperate.

* * *

Delfina woke, sweating, under the tree.

She looked around. She was still in the playground, which, no matter how one reimagined it, could never be the green plain of her dream. It was just a dusty city block bordered by equally four dusty streets, with a handful of trees scattered about, the swings and a bowl-shaped depression off to one side, beside which the local boys had built a couple of improvised soccer goals by piling some building stones on top of each other at opposite ends of a particularly bald and dusty stretch.

She breathed a sigh of relief and tried to will her heartbeat back under control. The wind picked up and stirred some loose pieces of bark around, making tiny dust devils over the stones.

Delfina checked her watch. It was just after six. She'd slept for nearly three hours, and now she felt alarm. What if the bus was early? She couldn't stand to stay another day in this hellhole.

She half-walked, half-ran to the traffic circle, arriving at six-twenty to find herself alone at the bus stop except for one woman who was seated on a bench under a shelter about ten yards from where the sign for Delfina's own bus was located.

The woman was dark-haired and appeared to be wearing coat that reached her ankles, despite the heat. She was looking in the opposite direction from Delfina, down the two-lane road along which the bus would likely come, which made it hard to guess her age, except that she seemed young.

Delfina sat and waited, checking and re-checking to see that she hadn't forgotten her bag or anything important. But no. Her purse held her DNI—her national identity document—and her wallet, which held a bit of cash, a debit card in her own name and, in case of complete and utter emergency, an extension of her dad's Visa card. That last, in particular, could bail her out of pretty much anything.

But using it would mean explaining herself, something she would hate to stoop to. She knew her parents would be glad to help her out, and they probably wouldn't even be openly critical of her life choices... but the sly little comments about useless poets and unsuitable young men would rankle. They might not know what she was really doing on her vacation, but they weren't dumb; they wouldn't be fooled into believing that a group of her girlfriends had abandoned her penniless somewhere in the wilds of Argentina's interior.

Still, it would be better to return with her head hanging low and her tail between her legs than not to return at all. It was a comfort to know that the card was there if she really needed it.

Time passed slowly. It appeared that six-thirty went on forever. She studied her watch to see if it had stopped, but it was ticking, and the second hand was moving. She looked around to see if there was a power outlet anywhere, where she could charge her phone. But this wasn't an airport. It was an outdoor bus station in the middle of nowhere.

Hell, the bus wouldn't have a charging port either, which meant she would need to wait until she got to the bus terminal at Salta itself before she could give any signs of life.

She shrugged. By definition, adventure had risk associated with it, and she would remember this fondly later in life, forgetting the anger she felt to become a story she could repeat over and over.

Even now, she wasn't frightened. The day was too warm to be frightening, and even though the shadows were lengthening, there were plenty of lights around the bus stop and the traffic circle.

Night fell quickly. It was still quarter before seven when the sun disappeared behind the mountains. She wondered at that, then remembered that, despite the heat, it was winter. She realized that summer would be seriously hot.

Seven o'clock came and went.

"Excuse me," she said to the other woman. "Excuse me."

The woman turned slowly and, for a moment, Delfina was terrified that her face would be a skull, a mass of tentacles, or some other horror-film cliché. Instead, a tired-looking woman in her twenties who might have been attractive if she hadn't been wearing so much makeup blinked at her, then looked around to see if there might be a mistake, if Delfina might have been talking to someone else.

"Yes?" the woman asked.

"I'm waiting for the bus to Salta," Delfina said. "They told me it comes at seven."

"Seven oh nine," the woman replied. "Sometimes a few minutes later."

Delfina glanced at her watch. It was only five past.

"Ah, thank you," she replied. Then Delfina waited for a few more minutes. "Do you know if the bus is ever this late?"

The woman shrugged. "I don't pay much attention to that, to be honest,"

"But… aren't you waiting for a bus, too? Don't you know the times?"

"I'm not waiting for a bus."

They sat in silence. Delfina on her bench, the other woman under the rest area roof. Finally, it got dark enough for the lights around the traffic circle to illuminate.

Wordlessly, the woman stood and removed her coat. Under it, she wore a day-glo orange miniskirt and a lacy white bra. High-heeled black boots with fishnet stockings completed the ensemble.

Noticing Delfina's stare, the woman looked back, her gaze an open challenge. "No women," she said, flatly. "I'm traditional that way."

Delfina shook her head. "I'm sorry. I didn't mean to be rude. And I'm definitely not judging you," she chuckled ruefully. "If you knew why I was out here…" She shrugged. "Anyway, I was wondering more about how many men you expect to see here in a night. You're the first person I've seen outdoors since I arrived in town."

The woman glanced upward, just a quick look, barely noticeable. She couldn't have seen much anyway, because the curved roof of the bus shelter would have hidden the emerging stars from view. "This is my place," the woman replied simply.

Delfina wondered what that even meant. Did it

mean that if she abandoned her post another woman would take it? Did it mean that her clients expected to meet her there?

She didn't know. She'd never spoken to a... a streetwalker... before. Delfina didn't know what to say to a person like that. She didn't want to offend the only other person in sight.

The woman must have known exactly what she was thinking. Must have thought her a hopeless innocent. "Go on. Ask," she said. "You know you want to."

"I... is it awful?"

The prostitute laughed. "No. Awful is living in this little town. Captured by the small minds that live in the past, so far in the past that they don't even know what century we're in. But my role... It's not better or worse than any of the others. I have a place in society. Everyone knows what my place is, and I know it, too. If I respect that place, and if others respect it, we have peaceful coexistence. If I try to move out of my circle, there is a ruckus." Then she laughed. "But not as much as when the grand women of town try to move into my circles. That's when things become truly scandalous." She cocked her head at Delfina. "I think you know what I mean."

Delfina imagined the reaction of her father's friends and neighbors if they ever found out the truth of what had happened here: the boy from the wrong social strata who'd treated her like his own personal high-class whore until he got bored, then abandoned her. And how she'd been perfectly happy to be a plaything. It wouldn't matter to the people judging her that he'd been a plaything that she'd used to feel powerful as well. In fact, it might make it worse. They could understand when a girl acted like a whore. What they would never understand was when a girl acted like a man.

The first was unfortunate, but common. You could brush it under the rug. Marry her off to an accommodating younger son with some stain on his own character. Whoredom happened. There was a long tradition of it. But a woman who looked at men the same way they looked at women? That was more disturbing. She would be shunned.

She wondered who had made the idiotic rules.

"I think I do. And I sometimes think the world I live in, the upper-class world of people with cell phones and CEO titles and international connections live in the eighteenth century."

The woman raised an eyebrow. "But that only matters when you step out of your role." She stared straight at Delfina. "Is your life so terrible that you need to live a different one?"

"No… but why shouldn't I have the things I want? Because my parents, or some priest, says so?"

"Because life doesn't work that way. Some people own the things. Others can only scrape a living from them." The prostitute looked around, saw that the dark road held no headlights, and sat with a sigh. "For example, the women of the town, the respectable women, they own my customers. I only get a living from borrowing them every once in a while. They are happy, their money makes me happy. And I can say I've been with the most powerful men in the region. Señor álvarez. Señor Sánchez de Guisada. Even the Colonel, Señor Peñaloza." She grunted. "The wives knew it, of course. But as long as I stay silent, they won't mention it and the balance remains undisturbed."

Delfina hesitated before speaking. There was something about those names that nagged at her, as if she should know them for some reason.

The prostitute stood again, walked to the edge of the shelter and back, like a lion in a zoo, pacing back and forth in its cage. Her movements were feline, too, aggressive, proud, as if daring anyone to challenge her. At each extreme of her walk, she would pose for a moment, as if showing herself off to an unseen army of leering men.

Then she'd turn and pace—four steps—in the other direction.

"What's your name?" Delfina asked.

The woman stared at her, surprised. "Why do you care?"

"I don't know. It just seemed we might be here a while. Both of us. And…"

"And you've never met a woman like me before."

"I haven't," Delfina replied. "But you seem to know more about me than I do myself."

"Not about you. About women like you. I grew up watching you, wishing I could be like you. I only realized the darkness hidden behind the finery when my… position meant I could peep behind the curtain." She smiled. "And all men are just little boys at heart. They all talk when they're in bed with a whore. They think the fact that they're paying you means you have to be a mother when you're not being a whore." She shook her heads. "And they hate their high-class wives. To a man, they hate them. They call them things you'd never repeat in society, they tell you what they'd do to them if they could. Because they are paying for my silence, too."

"My name is Delfina," Delfina said.

The prostitute nodded. "It means the chosen successor. Fitting." She laughed. "Don't look so surprised. I sell my body, but my mind is my own. I know a little of the French language."

"Don't you ever want to be something else?"

"I'm surprised you'd ask that. Haven't you learned that moving out of one's position only brings problems?"

"You can't really… wait, did you say Colonel Peñaloza? Does that family still live here? Wasn't there a Peñaloza who died here during the revolution? One of the Spanish loyalists?"

"He was a fat man. Not very well endowed. He paid good coin, Spanish coin, so that Pedro in the general store always knew when I'd been with the Colonel. He would grin and say that the Colonel's wife was always surprised when he gave her coins from Spain. She asked if the old man had been spending on spirits."

"Wait. The current Peñaloza? He pays in… Euros?"

"Of course not. There are no Peñalozas here now. I'm talking about the original one."

Delfina blinked. With dusk, the air had grown colder and water condensed around them. Little droplets mixed with the dust blown on the wind that swept the mountains from south to north and created a haze that reflected the lights from the traffic circle.

For a second, the light created the illusion that the woman speaking to her wasn't dressed in cheap clothes from the dregs of society's wet dreams, but in a flowing black dress, that was somehow equally gaudy and tawdry. By the time Delfina blinked away the tears from the grit in her eyes, the illusion had passed, and the woman standing there could have been an easy score in any modern nightclub, albeit one that would charge you for your victory.

The black eyes held Delfina's. "I gave my services to every man in town. The rich to keep myself in finery, the poor to keep myself in food. Estelita and I—Estelita was my main competitor, and also my only friend, even though the men preferred me, if I was free—knew what was going to happen. But how could we warn the loyalists? The men we would have betrayed if we told the rich men what was going to happen were our brothers, our cousins, our childhood companions. So I learned to do without finery." She looked down at herself. "As you've no doubt realized."

"I don't think the bus is coming," Delfina said.

"I suppose you're right," the woman replied.

"Goodbye." Delfina walked into the night, wondering if she should tell someone about the raving woman at the bus stop. Did she really think she was living in a ghost story?

But who could she tell? Who would care, in this tiny, traditional little town, that the local prostitute was slightly wrong in the head? Hell, that might be why she was the local prostitute. It might also explain why she attempted to ply her trade on a road without traffic.

Only when she reached the houses at the edge of town did she realize she never found out the woman's name.

For a moment, she considered going back to Joaco. To beg for his attention, or to steal his car keys, one or the other. But neither of those was going to work. The car had been borrowed from a friend. Could she really just take it?

Her feet decided for her. She stepped up to the

church and turned the handle. Her mind might be confused, but her body knew where she'd always felt safe as a child. Hours and hours spent in the church grounds, running around under the tolerant gaze of a succession of young priests who would later become important members of the San Isidro community.

Father Hermindez sighed, and she saw some of the air of put-upon patience she recalled from those priests of old.

"I hoped you wouldn't come here," he said. "But I knew you would."

Delfina blinked. "Were you expecting me to fight with Joaco?"

The priest stared at her. Somehow, his gaze made her think that the blind, milky eye was looking at her, too. She forced herself not to shudder. "No. I expected you to come ask questions," he said.

"I don't have questions," she replied. "I have too many answers I didn't want to face."

The priest sat heavily down on a bench on the first row of pews. The wood, dark and scarred with age, creaked. "Do you need a place to stay?"

"Only until the morning," she said. "I'm leaving as soon as the sun comes up. Do you know where I can hire a car, preferably with a driver?"

He shook his head. "We can figure it out in the morning. Are you hungry?"

"Oh, God no," Delfina replied. "I've already eaten too much today."

He nodded as if she'd expressed a profound truth. Then he shifted his weight on the bench. "You are Spanish, aren't you?"

Delfina cocked her head. "I was born in Buenos Aires," she replied.

"I mean your family."

"I suppose."

"All the way back?"

"Well, one branch is from the old stock. Varelas. The other branch… I think they were Martínez."

"A pure branch?"

"In what way, pure?"

"No Italian blood?"

Delfina tried to remember things she might have heard from her grandparents about the family history. Finally, she shrugged. "I don't remember any of that. I don't think so. We're just Spanish."

"And no native blood, either. No Englishmen, or Welsh grandmothers?"

"I don't really know."

The priest seemed about to say something, then looked away. "I don't have much to offer you in the way of accommodations. The church has only one room. That's where I normally sleep. You can have it."

"By no means. I'll sleep on one of the benches," Delfina replied. "As long as I have a roof over my head, I will be all right."

Father Hermindez didn't appear convinced, but he nodded. "As you wish. There is a small toilet just in that hall."

"Thank you."

"I generally go to bed early. I rise with the dawn to prepare for mass."

"Perfect. I'm exhausted," Delfina lied. She smiled, and he turned away with a mumbled "Good night."

When he left, Delfina allowed herself a shudder. The

man gave her the heebie-jeebies in a huge way. But at least the church had a power outlet in the back wall. She unplugged a tall fan and plugged in her phone, staring intently at it as it came back to life and showed the empty battery with a thin red line as the level of charge.

As soon as it came back to life, she tried to get a signal. No luck. Not even a wifi signal she could hop onto.

She cursed, but then remembered that she'd taken pics the day before. Hadn't she uploaded them onto Instagram? She checked.

Unable to upload, the window said.

Was this little town really so isolated? It didn't look that different from dozens of towns she'd been to. It certainly didn't feel any different. Just archaic and a bit underdeveloped. But not to the extent of not having cell phone coverage. Hell, you could get coverage on half the trails in mountains around Bariloche… It was ridiculous to think that a town in Argentina wouldn't have cell towers. Argentines were addicted to their phones, and the poorer the Argentine, the more addicted they were.

It made no sense, but she wasn't going to solve the mystery that night. She looked around.

The church was lit by a dim yellow bulb which swayed in a slight breeze coming in from high windows. Shadows danced around the room like living things.

Unable to decide whether etiquette would allow her to darken the room, and unwilling to disturb the priest, Delfina placed her bag on one of the benches, pressed herself against the backrest, and closed her eyes.

* * *

Two naked bodies thrusted at one another in the dancing light of the candle, casting grotesque shadows just like the ones she'd seen in the church.

The place smelled of stale sweat and the unmistakable tang of unwashed bodies, the smell Delfina had smelled countless times when passing a homeless man on the street. She looked around for the origin of the smell before realizing it had no particular source. It came from the room, and it came from the bodies.

Delfina tried to force herself to look away, to leave that room. She was no innocent when it came to sex, but had never derived much pleasure in watching others do it. Joaco had sometimes insisted that they turn on the video channels in the motels they frequented. And she either ignored them or asked him to turn it off. Porn just wasn't her thing.

Had it been, what she would have enjoyed certainly wouldn't have resembled the scene unfolding before her. A fat man pressed himself into a woman so much smaller than he was that she could barely be seen, except for a pair of legs sticking up into the air and a suggestion of black hair in the shadows. Folds of fat jiggled. The woman told the man how much she loved lying with him.

She's lying.

The thought struck Delfina with the power of absolute truth, and the realization gave her the strength to tear her eyes from the bed. The floor, a rough construct of widely-spaced planks that sagged into the dirt below, was covered with clothes.

Black pants, a white shirt and a wide hat appeared to

be the man's accoutrements, while the woman had worn a black dress, which might have once been elegant, but now lay in crumpled heap with signs of wear on the embroidery and small tears in the visible seams.

The dress made Delfina look up again. She'd seen it before.

Just as she did so, the man shifted, arcing up and moving his shoulder out of the way. Delfina got a look at the woman's face.

It was a face she knew. A face she'd seen minutes earlier.

The prostitute stared straight into her eyes, freezing Delfina with her gaze. Then, she smiled, looked away and moaned as if she was having the most divine experience of her life.

* * *

Delfina turned away. The hard backrest of the church pew halted the movement of her head.

"Ow," she said, rubbing her cheek.

Then she stood, grabbed a sweater from her bag, put on her shoes and headed back out into the night.

Streetlamps were few and far between in the little town, but it made no difference. There were no pedestrians to run into, no assailants waiting in the darkened doorways. She felt alone in the night.

Or at least alone except for natural things. She could sense scurrying creatures startled by her presence. A rustle of something between two stones, the snap of a twig in an empty lot.

She tried to remember whether there were any dangerous animals in those hills. Other than the possibility of a puma, which likely wouldn't be in the town itself, she couldn't think of anything.

The traffic circle was still illuminated. The night still tasted dusty and cool and humid. The prostitute still paced back and forth under the little roof. The woman watched as Delfina marched straight up to her, a tight, sardonic smile on her face.

"You saw me," Delfina said.

"You were dreaming," the prostitute replied.

Delfina stood, mouth agape. The other woman's smile broadened, but lost none of its sarcasm. "Or wasn't I supposed to know that?"

"It wasn't a dream, was it?" Delfina asked.

"Not for me, it wasn't. I tend to dream of pleasant things," the woman replied with a smirk. "But you have to admit I earned my keep." Now the laugh was genuine. "Oh, come on, woman. I was a whore. Do you think I talk like some little blushing debutante? Are you really so sheltered?"

"It was real. That was the colonel, wasn't it? I saw his portrait in the museum. He was that fat, balding man."

"It was."

"And it was real? It was two hundred years ago?"

"It was."

"What the fuck are you?" Delfina said.

"Ah. That's how I'm used to people talking to me." Then she shrugged. "I'm just a girl who had to work for her living. I miss those days."

Delfina had been standing on the street, not on the curb. The other woman hadn't left her shelter.

The noise of small animals behind her grew louder. Delfina turned to look. The prostitute followed her gaze. "You should probably get under the roof." She held out her hand.

Delfina hesitated. Was this woman a ghost? A demon? Some kind of hypnotist-cum-fraudster? If she took the woman's hand, would she turn into a ghoul and suck away Delfina's soul?

The smell of cheap perfume wafted across the distance between them, and Delfina decided she probably wasn't at risk.

She took the proffered hand, stepped onto the curb and, when nothing ate her soul, sat on the bench. "Can you tell me what's happening?"

"I don't know," the prostitute said. "Something in this town is wrong. But I don't know what. My memory isn't right. But I wear strange clothes, and I speak Spanish that I would never have used. Look at these colors. You say two hundred years. I can't even imagine why. I certainly can't remember two hundred years. But then, all of this around us…" Her gesture encompassed the highway and the traffic circle. "I know what it is, I know what a car is, and I know that if a car stops the man inside will take me to a cheap room and use my services, but I don't remember how I learned about them, or when all this was built. It just seems natural to me. As natural as horses used to seem. Or the first of the trains. Why do you say two hundred years?"

"Because that's how long ago, more than that, is how long ago it happened." Delfina studied the other woman. She didn't look like a ghost. No light filtered through her, the smell of the grave didn't follow her around. She looked utterly tawdry and terrene. Like a maid on her night off, looking for a good time.

Delfina immediately chastised herself for the

thought. She'd been brought up to see the poor as brothers and sisters in God. Her parents had always studiously observed that stricture, treating all their domestic staff—the live-in maid, the occasional nannies, the even-more-occasional gardener or plumber—as equals in every regard, people who gave of their time and effort in exchange for an agreed-upon wage. Just the way a young professional would when starting out in someone else's company. The fact that her friends were often disrespectful of the servant class didn't mean she could be. The guilt was so strong Delfina almost apologized for the unkind thought, before she remembered that the woman before her had already admitted to being a whore… the maids she needed to apologize to were not present. "Are you a ghost?" she said instead.

The prostitute stared out into the darkness, as if she saw—and feared—the source of the soft rustling. "I don't think so," she said. "I just want a customer."

"I haven't seen anyone outside. No men. No women. Certainly no one looking for sex." Delfina looked around. "And I'm going to find out why. Father Hermidez knows something." As soon as she said it, she was convinced it was true.

Delfina stood. She took two steps, but the prostitute's hand gripped her arm. "Don't go out there," she said.

"Why not? There's nothing out there."

"Can't you see them?"

"What?" Delfina asked. "It's just a few dogs. I'm going to find Father Hermidez. Come with me."

The other woman pulled back as if she'd been slapped. "No."

"Then I'm going without you."

The prostitute didn't let go. "They weren't dead," she whispered.

"What are you talking about?"

"When they went into the well. They weren't dead. And now they're out there!"

Delfina ripped her arm away and stepped back onto the street. The woman took a step after her, and it felt like the night suddenly went silent, as if the darkness itself had infinite eyes on the prostitute.

The woman must have noticed the change in the air because she yelped and stepped back, deep under the shelter, and sat on the bench. Then she looked up, surprised to see Delfina still there.

"You're one of them," the woman said. "Sent to lure me out. You're one of them."

The prostitute crossed herself and began to pray.

Delfina ran back the way she'd come.

* * *

Father Hermidez wasn't asleep. He was kneeling beside his bed when she burst into the room. He looked up at her.

"When I realized you were gone, I feared for your soul." He got slowly to his feet. "Now that you've returned, I realize it's mine that I should have been praying for."

"What is this place?" Delfina asked.

"Just a town."

"Bullshit."

She covered her mouth, more in surprise than shock. She'd never imagined she would talk to a priest that way.

Father Hermidez, however, didn't appear to care. His eyes downcast, he looked more like a little boy caught with his hands in the cookie jar than a figure of religious authority. "I thought I would be able to help," he said. "They ordered me not to come, and I thought they doubted my ability, like they always did. I thought they believed that a half-blind man couldn't do what was needed." He raised his face, and Delfina saw that tears rolled down his cheeks, that the blind eye was red, tiny veins visible in the milky nothing.

"What are you talking about?"

"The curse," Hermidez said. "I thought I could lift the curse. Bring the town back to the realm of the living. Give it a name."

"It has a name," Delfina replied. "I saw it on the map, above the town hall."

"Tell me what it is," the priest challenged.

"Carrizo."

"Perhaps. But the name has no meaning outside. Because it doesn't exist anymore. Your mind might think it has a name, but it's not there."

"Is any of this here?" Delfina asked, gesturing at the church. She walked back to the door and pulled it open. "Any of this?"

On the other side of the door, things watched. Each one was different. There were furry creatures with red, slavering maws. Malformed purple worms longer than a man was tall, hunched ghouls, pale skinned and emaciated.

The priest slammed the door shut.

"What the hell was that?" Delfina asked.

"That is what lives outside. They're trapped here

with us. In the town. The outside belongs to them, and we are only safe under a roof."

"I've been outside since I arrived."

"Perhaps you've been lucky. You must have remained in motion, keeping just one step ahead of them. Or maybe you spent most of your time in your room, with that young man…" The man said it hopefully, as he desperately needed Delfina to confirm it.

"Why would that be important?" she asked.

The priest looked away.

"Why won't anyone tell me anything?" she screamed at him.

"Because no one knows for sure what is happening. When I came, I rode a mule into the valley and walked off the road until I found the entrance to the town. Then I sat there and prayed for guidance. Nothing. Then, one day, I saw a shimmer in the distance, like a mirage from the heat, and I walked forward, and the town appeared around me. I've been here ever since, listening to the sounds of the night. I learned quickly that to emerge from under this roof meant death."

"There's a highway that comes in here," Delfina said.

"There wasn't when I arrived. That's progress, I suppose."

"When did you come in?"

"Just after the turn of the century." He smiled. "There was very little here then."

"In 2000? I find that hard to believe. The road I followed was older than that. The roads in the town are older than that," Delfina replied.

"Not that century," the priest replied with a sad smile. "I came here in 1902."

"I'm not stupid," Delfina replied. "You can't be more than forty."

"I feel much older than that. And then, at times, I feel I've only been in this town a few days. And yet, I'm surrounded by marvels." He pointed at the electric light and at her phone still plugged into the wall. "Marvels I've never learned about, and yet which feel natural to me. As if the town is caught in a bubble, always present, but with time never actually moving." He sobbed for a moment. "I can remember a hundred baptisms and a thousand funerals… and I can't remember who the people were. I've said a million masses, but I can't remember the complete words. I never could, which is another reason my superiors believed I would never amount to anything." He wept freely, openly, unashamedly. "They were right, and now I'm damned with the guilty and the innocent of a crime I only ever learned about through the garbled voice of memories I'm not sure are my own."

He rushed forward and grabbed Delfina's arm. The alcohol she smelled on his breath caused her to pull away. If he never left the church, where did he get the spirits to get drunk?

Father Hermídez stumbled towards her, arms extended, desperate expression on his face.

Forgetting what she'd just seen outside, Delfina ran from the things she knew about, the things she feared. In that moment, all she could see was her mother's face, sternly admonishing: "When men drink, the devil gets into them. Even good men. Stay out of their reach, or they'll overpower you. They'll rape you, and then the devil will be in you, too."

Her mother didn't believe in the devil; that was just

the kind of thing she said to make Delfina and her siblings sit up and take notice.

But the seven-year-old child who remembered the warning took over the twenty-year-old Delfina's body, and her instinct to flight took over and chose the nearest route out of immediate danger.

Delfina opened the door and stepped into the night.

"No!" the priest shouted. "Wait!"

The night surged around her as she suddenly remembered where she was, and what was out there with her, but she knew it was too late. She could never make if back inside before the creatures of the darkness swarmed over her. Already, she felt their acrid breath on her skin.

They surrounded her, monsters—albeit surprisingly small ones—from her nightmares. Most were short and squat, hairy and misshapen. Some were a little taller and thinner, as if they'd been squeezed into shape by a gigantic hand and then given scales and claws and teeth. A large, bulldog-shaped thing with skin that looked like raw meat and seeped blood onto the dirt floor stood before her.

They all stared up at Delfina, and in the looks, she saw humanity, even if the twisted forms were of assorted demons.

None of them touched her.

Not daring to move, barely daring to breathe, she turned to Father Hermídez. The priest crossed himself continuously, again and again and again. His lips moved at speed, and she could tell he was praying.

"Father, what can I do?"

He looked up at her. "I was right. I must pray for

myself, not for you. He held up a crucifix as if it would somehow affect her. She looked at it, bemused.

The priest made a soft, keening sound, and fumbled with the door, finally getting it closed on his third attempt. The door blocked the yellow light from within.

Delfina stood on the threshold, immobile. Without the light from the church, the monsters had faded back into the night, but she could still feel their warmth, smell their stench. Most of all, she could feel their gaze on her.

She fought to control her bladder, holding in the scream that desperately wanted to escape as she waited for the first bite, that gnawing on her ankle that would precede the full-blown attack which would tear her to shreds.

It didn't come. If anything, she felt the night moved away and that the creatures had retreated, leaving her space to see what she would do.

Joaco, she thought.

She began to walk towards Doña Julia's house, but when the entire night seemed to come with her, a darker blackness within the night, she abandoned decorum and ran.

The door to the street was locked.

She banged on the green wood, screamed to be let inside, but there was nothing she could do. Finally, in fury, Delfina pulled a municipal trash canister onto the sidewalk, climbed on, and scaled the wall.

She dropped into the garden, which shook and creaked as if the entire army of the night had entered with her. She pushed her way through the trees until she made it to the grass. There, the light from the room she'd shared with Joaco shone onto the garden.

He was sitting where she'd left him, head bowed over the paper, visage screwed up in concentration.

When Deflina stepped onto the covered porch that ran the length of Doña Julia's house, two things happened at once: the creatures of the night, the ones she felt more than actually saw, stopped as if they'd hit a solid wall; and Joaco looked up from his writing.

He looked straight into her eyes. "So. This is how it is," he said.

"Joaco, I need help," she replied.

"I think you have all the help you'll ever require," he replied.

Then, for the first time since he sat down, Delfina saw him move. He stood, leaned forward and, with slow, deliberate movements, closed the shutters.

"What? No!" Delfina screamed. She banged her fists against the wood, tried to peek through the cracks, yelled until her voice was hoarse. But she could see him inside, unperturbed, filling page after page with the tripe he called poetry. "I'll rip his balls off," she said.

Delfina rushed to the door and pulled down on the handle, but it was locked as well. Banging on it did no better than attacking the shutter had. Nothing stirred in the house.

Exhausted, she turned away.

The night, dark and hungry, stared back from the garden. She couldn't see the individual horrors from where she stood, but she could feel the night moving, feel its collective heart beating.

"God," she sobbed. Tears exploded from her, all the grief and horror and confusion emerging in a single anguished cry which made her knees turn to water. She sat heavily on the stoop, and cried into her hands, her sobs echoing from the little roof over the entrance. She had nowhere to go, no one to turn to, so she cried for her mother, for her God, for anyone who could help her, even though she knew no one would answer the call.

She cried until she had no more strength to cry. Yelled until all that emerged were hoarse shouts. Then she put her head on her knees and hoped to disappear.

She didn't disappear. She looked up into the waiting night to see that a piece of darkness had detached itself from the inky mass.

The creature advanced toward her. Very little light reached their position, but in that light, Delfina thought she could see a man-shaped—albeit twisted and deformed—entity about half her height. It had an elongated head which palely reflected the light, showing facets as if it had scales. Large, reptilian eyes protruded from the side of its head, and long teeth emerged from the mouth at all angles. Some liquid—drool, blood, something even more disgusting—leaked from the gaps between the teeth.

It approached to just where the edge of the little roof protected her head from rain and stopped.

It held out a short, scrawny arm, claw extended.

At first, Delfina thought it was trying to see whether it could grab her, but being thwarted by the mystical power of the roof over her head. But there was something about that gesture...

"You want me to go with you?" she said.

The creature grunted and stretched towards her

before pulling back with a hiss of pain. Then it reached out again, more carefully.

Delfina reflected that if anyone had told her she would take the hand of a misshapen monster, part of a horde of demons, on a dark night in the middle of nowhere, she would have laughed at them. She'd have angrily accused them of calling her stupid.

She chuckled darkly at the thought and extended her hand.

The claws felt warm and dry.

* * *

The dark monster tugged, obviously urging her to follow. Delfina stood and allowed herself to be led.

A lamb to the slaughter, she thought. *But what other choice do I have? Besides, better to get slaughtered quickly than to end up like that priest. Or that poor, sad whore, stuck forever under the dubious protection of a bus shelter, not even certain what forever means.*

She walked beside the monster. The energy among its unseen companions appeared to have intensified. She thought she could feel a buzz in the garden, the sense of anticipation, of hunger.

Delfina had the sense that she would be the main course in a long-anticipated feast.

They walked the streets and, for the first time since she'd arrived, she thought she saw people. A shadow of a woman there, in a hooped dress and a large hat. A man carrying boxes that, one moment appeared to be cardboard, the next a slat-sided wooden box filled with apples. Two boys in white shirts tormenting an invisible dog.

As soon as she focused on an apparition, it faded, to

be replaced by another hovering in the corner of her eye. Even the monster leading her by the hand faded at times so she could feel him but not quite make him out, except when they were directly under a streetlight.

But the thing's tug never weakened.

It appeared to prefer the darkest streets, the ones without too many cables overhead, and it seemed to be heading straight towards the playground…

…which wasn't there when they arrived.

Delfina looked around at the dark, empty field. The lights were even dimmer here than elsewhere in the little town, and she stood for a moment, completely certain that she'd gotten turned around, that she was somewhere else.

Where the little depression should have been stood a well, surrounded by a little wall of yellow stone. A bucket lay on its side next to it. The swings were nowhere to be seen.

The tug on her hand grew more urgent. She followed as if in a dream. It had to be a dream, didn't it? The things she saw around her didn't exist in real life. Not in the 21st century. Hell not even in the past, when people believed in that kind of crap.

Now, she stood by the well.

Delfina bent to look inside.

Something pushed her in.

* * *

Delfina screamed and dodged as she nearly hit her head against the far edge of the well. She reacted instinctively and only realized too late that she should have grabbed onto the opposite side.

Now she braced herself to hit… what? Would this

old well still have water in it, or would she slam into the ground to break every bone in her body.

Something brushed her arm, a spiderweb, or a tendril of root.

Another touched her leg.

Within moments, Delfina felt the touches begin to slow her fall. None of them were strong, and she couldn't grab onto anything, but there were so many that it seemed the air itself had grown too thick for her to fall through.

Her feet made contact with the bottom, not to push through and sink into putrid water or to break her legs into splinters, but to land on a path covered in some feathery substance. She knew it was a path because she could see it extending into the distance; tunnel walls just wide enough to allow her to pass without brushing her shoulders glowed green. At the far end, a soft, salmon-colored glow marked what she thought had to be her destination.

She walked, the tug on her hand now gone, the only sound the echo of her footsteps against the walls. The tunnel smelled musty.

The path opened up. For a moment, Delfina thought she saw a mass of bodies piled up against each other as new ones came in from above to crush those already there. Whispered screams floated through the room.

Then the darkness receded. As light entered the room—two candles on a table came to life—she found herself in a circular chamber of rock. This wasn't the ubiquitous rock of the surrounding countryside: yellowish stone that looked like it would wear away quickly. This was dark grey rock. Serious rock. The kind you'd use to build a fortress at the top of a mountain if you needed to hold a pass for the next five thousand years. It was rock that would last.

A raised dais dominated the room. A throne, occupied by a rotund man was the only thing on the platform.

"Hello, Colonel," Delfina said.

The man studied her in silence, then grunted. "You have been talking to fallen women," he said. His voice, neither too high or too low, seemed to resonate with the rocks of the wall, making the chamber vibrate like they were caught inside a bell. "It's not seemly for a woman of good blood, much less an unmarried woman, to speak with such as her. You learn things you should never know."

"I don't think that woman was the source of the things I've seen. She is just caught here. Like me."

"None of us controls our destiny," the colonel said.

The figure on the throne flickered, and the rotund, mustachioed features were replaced by a severe, thin woman with a nose like an axe-blade and dark, piercing eyes. She sniffed. "It's quite a pity that you were the only one to come to us. I don't think you are suitable."

"Suitable for what?" Delfina asked.

"To untie the knot. To fulfill your destiny." The woman looked her over. "Perhaps it's for the best. It is perhaps best that this task is done by someone not too pure."

"I don't know what you're talking about."

The face morphed again. The severe woman was replaced by a round-faced youth. "They murdered us. Just because we thought differently from them."

"The townspeople? It was a revolution. A war. They were defending themselves," Delfina replied, remembering the exhibit in the town hall. "And besides, that was two hundred years ago. The town has changed. The people in it probably aren't even descended from the ones you killed. But even if they were, you can't seek revenge for something that happened in a war."

"Lies! All lies!" A little girl with pale white skin looked back at Delfina from the throne. "They called the men to a peace conference, under the banner of truce. When the men arrived, they attacked them. And when they surrendered, they tied them up and threw them into the well."

A young woman replaced the girl. "Then they came for the wives and daughters. Drunk men, dirty men. They did what men do to unprotected women. Then they threw us into the well. Alive."

"Don't tell us about not wanting revenge." The colonel had returned. His skin burned, red.

"But it isn't the same people. Perhaps some are descended… but I doubt it. A town like this will have changed completely in that much time."

"Time," another man had taken the colonel's place, "Does not flow here as it does in other places."

"Of course it does. I walked through the town. It looks like any other tiny place in the Argentine interior," she said. "I bought a bottle of water out of a refrigerator in a *kiosco*. Are you going to tell me you had plastic bottles when this happened to you?"

A young man with a goatee looked out at her. "We know little of these things," he said. "What you say might be true. Or perhaps you are lying. Or perhaps you are simply confused. What we know is that every soul living here is one of the people…"

The body changed again to show the faces of

everyone she'd already spoken to and many, many people she didn't recognize.

"…who murdered us."

"I'm not."

"No. And neither is that man you came here and sinned with," the hatchet-faced woman was back. "But he is nothing, polluted, impure. Worthless."

"From your words, so am I," Delfina replied.

"Your actions may leave much to be desired," the colonel said. "But your blood is of the best. Not a drop of lesser worth courses through your body." The multitude returned. "We can feel it."

"What…" Delfina began. Then she caught herself. "Is that what Father Hermidez was going on about?"

The figure on the throne hissed. "That man has been trying to send us to hell since he arrived. He is too stupid to understand that we aren't the ones that belong in hell. That he should send his precious flock there. That is where they send murderers and rapists and half-breeds."

Delfina chuckled in spite of herself. "Wow, you really aren't a very politically correct group of ghosts, are you?"

The colonel returned. "You don't believe us." It wasn't a question.

Delfina shook her head. "Either this is a dream, or I've completely lost my mind. But either way, there is nothing to be gained from taking it too seriously."

"You are our only hope," the man on the throne said.

She couldn't help but remember him grunting on the prostitute. "Then you have no hope."

The severe lady returned. "I think you don't quite understand."

And suddenly the room around Delfina disappeared. She lay on her face in the dark, pain radiating from her left arm. She tried to lift herself into a sitting position, but gasped in agony. She was lying on something soft, and when she poked at it, a man grunted in wordless agony.

She didn't have time to investigate. From above her, a high-pitched yell echoed and something hit Delfina in the small of the back with near-bonebreaking force. She gasped and jerked, and the pain from her arm brought stars to her vision.

"Mamá," a tiny voice said. "It hurts. Mamá. My legs, mamá."

The child's voice made Delfina forget her own pain. She reached out to try to find the child's head and comfort it, but as she reached out, something large slammed into her outstretched good arm. It snapped like a twig.

Now Delfina found herself pinned under the new body. Another woman, squirming and crying. Delfina tried to get the woman's weight off of her, but movement hurt so much she forced herself to lie still. It was hard to breathe, but it was better than the pain.

A thud above increased the pressure on her chest. A woman cursed and wailed for god to save her.

Another child rained down, crying all the way.

Delfina realized she was in the well, the men beneath her, the rest of the women and children being thrown in after.

Someone landed, and though this impact hit the people already piled on top of her, Delfina felt the woman above her press harder into her throat. She fought to move her head from the crushing weight as she fought to breathe. Her only consolation was the conviction that she would suffocate soon, and the problem would end.

Another body fell. Another. More and more, and each increased the crush. She breathed desperately, in gasps, half praying that the weight would somehow be lifted, half hoping that she would just die once and for all.

She wanted to scream, but she couldn't do more than take the shallowest of breaths. The pain in her arms was there, but forgotten in the much greater agony of barely being able to breathe.

Finally, her chest could do no more against the crushing weight, and darkness overcame her.

Delfina…

…found herself on the floor of the large round room, panting on her hands and knees, simply glorying in the sense of air, blessed air pouring into her lungs. She looked up to see that the throne was occupied by every person at once, looking back at her.

"That's what they did to us," the voice of every Spanish loyalist who'd lived there in 1810 told her. "That's what they condemned innocent women and children to feel. As well as men who'd done nothing to harm them except to own land and give them jobs. They clothed everything in revolutionary words, but the truth was greed and murder and rape."

"And one of them even told me," a dark-eyed beauty informed Delfina, taking the body for herself, "that he would spare me if I agreed to marry him. I told him he was like dirt beneath my boots. He knocked me down on the floor and took me right there. Then he called his friends. When they finished, they threw me into the well, naked as the day I was born."

"I didn't die right away," a girl of ten said. "I landed on the very top of the pile. My baby brother and I died of thirst. I tried to rip open my veins so he could drink. But I couldn't do it. All I had were my teeth, and I couldn't bring myself to do it."

Delfina struggled to her feet. "What do you want from me?"

The grey-haired, steel-eyed woman returned. "Do your duty," she said.

"Do your duty," the colonel echoed.

"Do your duty," a little girl said in words that were slightly slurred, almost baby talk.

"What duty? I'm just a regular woman. I don't owe you anything."

"Your blood says differently. You are pure of blood, and therefore pure of heart. And you have no choice. You are a warrior of Spain by virtue of that purity. The only warrior we have."

"I'm no warrior. Guns scare the hell out of me," Delfina said.

The colonel reappeared. "Your words hold no import. You are the only person of trustworthy blood to come to us since we fell. Moreover, the spirits of our people at war have already visited you... the first time in memory that has happened." Then he smiled, a genuine smile, not the evil grin that she would have expected from the long-dead ghost of a colonial oppressor. "And this battle is not one of guns. You will see."

"I won't. I want no part of this." Delfina turned to look back the way she'd come. There must be a way to climb back up the well. To call for help. The modern people of the little town wouldn't ignore that, would they?

She started to turn, but before she'd even gotten halfway, a ghostly light emerged from the wall and impaled her. For a moment, she stood motionless, the light going through her, emerging from her back as if Delfina was a giant prism. She stifled a scream.

The light disappeared, and she collapsed to her knees again.

Fire coursed through her veins. Electricity seemed to jump between her fingers when she held her hand aloft. Every nick and scratch, every vestige of the exhausting days she'd suffered, was gone. She felt like she could run a marathon and box a heavyweight champion at the end of it. And win. By a one-punch KO in the first round.

Not waiting to see what else the spirits of the Spanish dead would do to her, Delfina ran back the way she came. She barely touched the walls of the well as she ascended. She shot past the mouth, to arc in the air and land solidly on her feet.

Behind her, the well disappeared, replaced by the dusty lot with the swings and the soccer field. She recognized the mortared rocks that had been pushed into place as goalposts: those were stones from the well.

Delfina decided she was going to leave the town. If necessary, she would walk all the way to Salta.

Hell, the way she was feeling, a little walk of a hundred kilometers or so would do little more than give her a healthy appetite.

As soon as she took the first step, she was back in the well. Not in the chamber, but under the press of bodies, suffocating. The memories were of a different person this time: a man who'd been knifed in the preceding fight and was dying faster from blood loss than lack of air.

The vision lasted only for a moment, but she understood what had happened. The vengeful spirits were inside her. Their lives, and especially their deaths were a part of Delfina's essence… and they could use that presence to control what she experienced.

The message was clear: *do what we ask or live forever under the growing weight of bodies in a well. Die in the most horrible way, over and over again.*

Delfina walked in a daze. Instead of going to Salta, she decided to visit the prostitute. The woman was worldly. She would have some kind of answer.

As she walked, she lost herself in the memories she'd gained so suddenly.

* * *

…the dead men had been thrown, unceremoniously, into the well. The water would be poisoned forever, but Don Tomás de Mendoza had more pressing problems.

He looked up to see the townspeople arrayed before him, expectant. The colonel was unconscious. Sebastián was dead. That left Tomás as the most respected of the patrones, of the leaders of the community. He straightened and looked Güiraldes straight in the eye.

"What you've done is an atrocity. We came here in good, Christian faith to discuss things like civilized people and you attacked without warning. You're no better than animals."

He hadn't meant to antagonize the man. This little half-breed had always had airs above his station, wanting to be treated like a Spaniard despite having been abandoned by his disgraced mother as soon as he was quit of her body. He was always in a foul mood, none fouler than when he smiled.

Güiraldes was smiling now, but Tomás couldn't bring himself to fear the man. You didn't fear your servants or lackeys. They might murder you for your gold teeth if they had the numbers, but they could never command that you feel anything but contempt for them. Even when they came at the head of a mob.

He held Güiraldes' eye and, to Tomás satisfaction, the little bastard looked away first.

A commotion in the back of the silent, sullen crowd of laborers and field hands died down quickly, and Güiraldes spat and moved aside to reveal old Tierca, the madwoman who lived halfway up the cerro and to whom the Indian girls went for love potions, and then went to again when the love was consummated and their bellies began to swell... with the man probably a hundred leagues away.

The crone glared at the men and nodded in satisfaction. She spat as well, her saliva turning to mud in the dirt of the common area.

"You'll never find rest," she said. "I curse you. I curse your family. I curse your very race and every member of it that sets foot on our lands."

Tomas felt a shiver run down his spine. "You ignorant hag," he said. "Take back your curse or suffer for it. The people of this place have always acted with piety and propriety, never taking more than their due or working our servants any harder than pity allowed. If you must kill us, let us go to our reward and disturb you no longer. Our God will shelter us."

The woman spat again. "Never shall you know any shelter save the dark places under the earth and the shadow of night. That is my curse."

"Then this is mine," Tomás replied. Ignoring the woman, he looked straight into the eyes of the coward Güiraldes. "My curse is that the crone's malediction have the same adverse effects as her love potions. People as ignorant as you are deserve to have your wishes come true." He spat beside where the others had.

Something hit Tomás in the back of the neck and he nearly collapsed onto the floor. Nerveless, the world swimming in his sight, he was dragged to the edge of the well, and then over.

He fell...

* * *

...the colonel lifted himself from between little María's spread legs and looked at her. No more than an animal, really, nothing like the women you could hire when you stopped in Tucuman.

But she was what the town offered, so it was what he took. He dropped a couple of coins onto the floor, and she scrambled for them.

"It's ten times what you're worth," he told her.

"Thank you, thank you."

He walked out.

* * *

Doña Ubenza, the colonel's wife, adjusted her severe grey bun when she heard his horse clatter up the lane. She watched him dismount and waddle up the path with the self-satisfied air of a man who'd visited the town whore.

She didn't even need to smell the perfume on the air around him, or the stale odor of that woman—old sweat and the reek of other men—to know that this time he'd been with Maria, not Estelita. He always came back full of himself when he fucked Maria. According to the other women, Estelita demanded that the men respect her, that they pay upfront, and that they speak to her with gentility. When he came back from her, he acted almost like a chastised schoolboy.

When he came back from María, he swaggered like a sailor after his first drink ashore, bursting with unspent pay.

"Good afternoon, my colonel," she greeted him stiffly.

"Good afternoon, my sweet," he replied with a big smile. He patted her gently on the shoulder as he swept past.

Definitely María today, Doña Ubenza thought.

* * *

Carmelita cried. "But he's my friend."

"No. He isn't. He's the peon's son," her mother admonished sternly. "You can't play with him anymore."

"I like playing with him. He's the only one who likes to play in the fields. All the other girls and boys are too old. Or too little, like baby Nuria."

"I've heard enough. Go off to bed and heed what I told you. I don't want to hear that you've been running wild with the servants."

Carmelita obeyed.

Then she cried herself to sleep.

* * *

The prostitute looked up. "I see you're back," she said simply.

"Not alone."

The woman—María, Delfina realized—looked around. "I don't see anyone. Less than usual, even, which is strange, as normally, I have to share the night with all sorts of monsters and deformities."

Just let us in. Cross the threshold. The roof. Walk across the place where the roof divides shelter from the unsheltered, the voices in her mind screamed.

"Give me a minute," she said.

"What?" María cocked her head at him.

"Why didn't you tell the colonel about the plot to kill them? You were the one person who could have saved them. A single word in his ear when you were alone, and none of this would have happened. The handful of Spanish loyalists here wouldn't have made any difference to the outcome of the revolution."

María glared at her. "I did it because he always treated me like nothing more than a piece of meat. He deserved what he got."

"And the women and children?" Delfina demanded.

"If you saw how the women treated me… us… I can understand pretending a whore doesn't exist. But they treated everyone who wasn't pure Spanish exactly the same way: like we were things put on Earth to serve them."

Delfina felt the anxiety within. *Go. Go now. We want her. Cross the line.*

"What will you do to her?" Delfina asked.

The prostitute cocked her head, studying Delfina.

The ghosts inside her said nothing. Instead, they gave her just the tiniest sense of being stuck in the well shaft.

Delfina swallowed and stepped forward. The air under the roof of the bus shelter resisted her. She needed all her newfound energy to break the plane, as if she was pushing against a giant sheet of transparent plastic.

She broke through and stumbled forward a couple of steps.

As Delfina struggled through the unseen barrier, the prostitute's expression turned from a mix of apathy and the slightest tinge of curiosity at Delfina's antics, to surprise and then, with a sudden burst of realization, terror. She took a step back. Then another. Then she stopped: a third step would have moved her out from beneath the protection of the roof.

For her part, Delfina felt elation course through her when the resistance collapsed and she entered the little rectangle defined by the roof. The emotion wasn't hers, but she felt its effects. It was like winning the lottery or meeting the guy of her dreams: she could have walked on air.

Two dark wisps of smoke emerged from Delfina. As the process wasn't painful, Delfina watched, more bemused than frightened as the tendrils took shape and became solid forms. Two of the monsters she'd seen—a boar-shaped, grunting thing that could only be the colonel and a snake-like shape that ended in powerful tentacles.

They advanced on the screaming prostitute. Slowly, savoring their moment. Delfina tried to find the colonel's memories, but where they would have been were only the faintest recollections. The man was no longer present in the roiling turmoil within.

María screamed as the two shadowy forms advanced on her. Delfina watched, fascinated, wondering what the phantoms would do. Would they enter her mind and suffocate her with memories of the calvary in the well? Would they overcome her, take over her body to live out the lives that had been so brutally cut short?

The tentacled monster came into range first, and launched itself at the cowering figure of the prostitute.

One of the tentacles wrapped itself around her arm. Another around an ankle. And it began to pull, stretching her body like some medieval torture device.

María's screams of terror turned into yells of pain. Delfina heard a shoulder pop out of place, or perhaps it was a knee. She couldn't tell from where she stood.

Delfina wanted to turn away, to run and hide from the knowledge that she'd been the one to cause this, made it possible for the monsters to get their revenge.

The boar-like monster, inky black, grunted and joined the fray. Its methods were less complicated. Jagged teeth tore into the prostitute's side, staining the once-slutty clothes into gore-spattered rags.

And still the woman screamed. Apparently, the fact that revenge had been delayed for hundreds of years didn't mean they would rush to exert that revenge.

They took their time. The tentacles stretched slowly, accompanied by pops and groans. The razor-sharp teeth only raked and tore at unimportant parts of the anatomy, avoiding major arteries.

The woman screamed and screamed.

At one point, she showed a moment of lucidity.

Overcome by the sheer effort of screaming continuously, her head lolled to one side and her wide-open, terrified eyes made contact with Delfina's. "Save me," the woman said.

Fury rose inside Delfina. Again, she realized the emotion wasn't her own but that of the ghosts within.

She shook her head. Her mouth moved almost on its own—still under Delfina's control, but motivated by the overwhelming anger inside. "You could have saved them. You knew. And you let them die. I can't save you. But even if I could, I'm not certain I would. Little children."

"I didn't know they'd kill the children."

"You should have thought. You knew what the townspeople were like. Resentful. Angry. Unfeeling. You could have prevented this."

But María screamed again as the boar bit into the nether regions, savaging the anatomy that had given him pleasure during his lifetime.

"No!" she screamed. "Help."

But no help was forthcoming. Her fate had been sealed two centuries earlier, and she'd spent the intervening time in a purgatory whose final and inevitable destination wasn't heaven but hell.

Delfina could see the separation in her shoulder now, under tension from the tentacles. It looked like the arm had to come off completely at any moment.

But, weakened by the colonel's bites, it was actually the left leg that gave way first, coming free with a pop and a sudden rush of blood.

The screams fell to a whisper, then ceased altogether as María, too weak from blood loss, fell silent. Within moments her eyes filmed over and the tension of pain disappeared from her body.

The monsters, however, weren't done yet. The tentacled monster finished pulling away every limb. The boar kept biting, tearing, grunting.

When they finally turned away from the corpse, there was nothing left of the woman who'd been María but a pool of blood and viscera, a red pile of bits and pieces unrecognizable as anything human. Even the face and hair had been gnawed away and the skull crushed like a nut.

Their grisly task completed, the two monsters made no attempt to return to Delfina. They just disappeared into the night.

* * *

Delfina watched the colonel's host body disappear from the little oasis of light around the traffic circle.

"Is that it? Are we done?"

A storm of emotion welled up inside her, and the image of the well flashed before her eyes.

"I guess not," she said. "So, what? The colonel is gone. He was your leader."

This time, the emotion was amusement, and another memory—she was beginning to recognize them—came, unbidden, to Delfina.

* * *

A full-length mirror supported by a wooden base showed the image of a naked woman, a woman Delfina recognized as the colonel's wife. Her hair was streaked with grey, true, but as it fell along her shoulders in curls, released from the tight bun she normally wore, it softened her stark features.

Delfina saw that the woman must have been around forty, perhaps younger, and quite handsome with her features correctly framed.

Likewise, her body was impressive—soft curves underpinned by the strong muscles of a woman accustomed to walking and to doing her own heavy lifting—and it was covered with skin of the palest milk-white, untouched by the sun. A sensual, unexpected physique.

"Are you finished admiring yourself?" a voice asked. "Your husband will be back soon."

The colonel's wife turned to look at the man who'd spoken. He was also in his forties, trim and muscular, but not pale. He was a man who worked outdoors, not shunning the sun or allowing himself to go to seed. He sat, legs immodestly open on the bed she shared with no one else, in the room her husband never entered.

"He won't be back until nightfall," she replied. "Unless the tavern runs out of drink or the whores refuse to spread their legs. In the meantime, Don Estanislao steals his cattle and brands them for himself."

"That isn't true," the man on the bed replied. Delfina recognized him, now: it was Tomás, the man who'd defied the murderers to his last breath.

"It should be. My husband is a wastrel and a coward, who believes that a military title his family bought for him entitles him to respect and position." She spat. "A man who can't even keep his own wife from shaming him with another man."

"I feel no shame in this," Tomás said. "And I don't think you do, either."

"You have no reason to feel shame. It is I who will burn in hell forever because I broke my wedding vows."

"I do not believe that God would punish you for an indolent husband. You are more faithful to him than he is to you. You keep his affairs in order and keep yours secret. If it wasn't for the way you've managed his business in his absence, he would be a pauper, and you would be back in Zaragoza with your family and well rid of him. If anyone is to rot in hell, it will be the colonel, who ruts with the village whores and drinks his days away, and dœs so in view of god and the entire town."

"God sees all, Tomás."

"And he judges fairly. You will not burn."

"Will you be there to help me face my judgment?"

"Haven't I been here for you every time you needed assistance? With your house? With your fields?"

"Help me face my judgment."

"I will."

Saying no more, the colonel's wife walked over to the bed and straddled her lover.

* * *

The demons within Delfina took her to the church next.

"Why are we even going there? The father wasn't part of the mob that murdered you."

The messages that came back were garbled bits of memory, snatches of conversation and the sense that the priest had to be removed. That was followed by an admonition in the form of the now-familiar crushing weight of bodies in a shaft.

"All right. But let me handle this. Do you absolutely need to tear him apart?"

A sense of ambivalence was her only answer.

"All right. Then don't come out. I'll handle it."

The church door was locked, and the priest refused to open it when she knocked. She walked around the little chapel. But there were no other entrances unless she decided to break a window.

The creatures within grew restless, so she returned to the door and pushed.

The strength of an entire town filled her, and the door opened with almost no resistance as the age-hardened wood splintered.

The sound of feverish, panicked praying came from within.

"Oh, stop it. I'm not going to hurt you," she shouted.

"What?"

"I said I'm not going to hurt you. Now show yourself."

A dark closet between the altar and the door to the priest's room shook and opened. The priest unfolded himself from within and stood, shame mixed with mistrust on his features. "Are you alone?" he said, staring around the room as if trying to pierce the shadows with his blind eye.

"No," she replied. "But if you do as I say, you will only have to deal with me."

"Do you swear to it by the power of God who lives within this hallowed ground?"

"No," Delfina said again. "But if you don't trust me, I'll leave you to explain it to the ones who've come with me. I've already seen what happens to those they encounter." She looked at him critically for several moments. "I don't think your soul is ready for what would happen to you in that case. I think, perhaps, you know that you have done less than you could have."

The priest swallowed. He looked around again. Finally, with the air of a man heading to the gallows, he stepped forward.

It took him quite a while to cross the church and reach the door.

And even then, he hesitated on the threshold.

"Hurry or I'll leave you here with the things accompanying me."

Still, he hesitated.

"Oh, for Christ's sake," Delfina said, and she pushed the priest out of the door, wondering what had become of those towering authority figures she remembered from her youth, those men whose wisdom was only matched by their courage in saying what needed to be said and doing what needed to be done.

The man stood stiffly, trembling beside the door of his church, the church that had held him prisoner for decades. He looked into the night and shuddered.

"There's nothing out there," Delfina said. "And now you have a choice. We will allow you to leave this place. Walk straight out of the town to the main highway, and you will live. That is a promise from me and from everything you fear." She walked around and stood in front of him. "Or you could stay here and do the job you should have been doing since you arrived. The job you promised God to do."

And she understood why the priest had to leave. All it would have taken was a single blessing, the right words over the well, to consecrate the bodies and turn the grave into a Christian burial—and to annul the curse of the old witch-woman. The souls inside her had decided to forego their Christian rewards for the sake of revenge.

Worse, he could say the right words over the bodies of the people who would fall this night, and that would be unacceptable. The shades within her wanted those souls to remain in limbo for centuries like they had.

The priest could still affect the outcome.

But he hurried off into the darkness, at the fastest speed his legs—legs that had been used only to walk from one end of the church to the other for whatever warped period of time he'd actually been confined—allowed.

She watched him leave, taking all her hope with him.

* * *

A memory.

Delfina was inside another woman. A young woman, to judge by her mode of dress. A man approached her on a path beside a river.

The halfwit, Delfina's host thought. Delfina felt her desperately search for a way out, to find an alternative path that wouldn't force her to walk past the man. Spotting none that wouldn't have meant abandoning decorum, she gritted her teeth and proceeded on her path.

"Hello, Señorita Hacienda," the man said, removing the dirty rag he called a cap. Had he not been soft in the head, he would have been quite pleasant to look at. Years of the hardest labor—the only labor he was fit for—had turned his arms into thick cords of muscles.

She looked away. "Hello, Ramón," she replied.

Though she knew better, she pretended the

conversation was over, that they'd merely exchanged pleasantries, but he shifted his position just slightly, in that way he had, and stopped her progress.

"My voices... the ones I told you about... they've been talking."

"That must be interesting," she replied.

"They speak of you."

A wave of revulsion coursed through her and, despite the indignity of it, she tried to push past him. He smelled of manure.

Ramón did the unthinkable: he reached out and took hold of her arm.

Fury pushed aside the revulsion. "What do you think you're doing?" she said in the iciest tone she could muster.

He let go of her arm as if she were a hot coal. "I'm just trying to warn you. The voices say that you need to get out of this place. To ride as far and as fast as you can go, or tomorrow you will die in a deep, dark place."

She brushed past him. Only when she was far enough away that he couldn't capture her again did she turn back to him. "In the first place, you will never dare touch me again. Never. Do you understand?"

She waited until he nodded dumbly.

"Good. And as for your voices, they are nothing. Just something wrong with your head. Your mother probably dropped you when you were a child. You're not right, and everyone in the village knows it. They laugh at you."

Then she walked away, and thought no more of it until the following day when a group of whooping men rode up to her house. Her father and brother had gone to a parley with the townsfolk, and she'd been left alone with her mother and the servants.

A crashing noise from the front of the house was followed by the strident tones of her mother asking what was happening.

When her mother's demands turned to screams, she knew something was wrong and began to fear for her life.

Her room offered little place to hide, and before she could escape to a more suitable spot, four men burst into her chamber.

Ramón led them, a whirlwind of violence that burst into her room and quickly immobilized her. As he tore her dress off, he said, apologetically: "I tried to warn you."

She tried to beg, to plead, to threaten him, anything that might induce him to let her go, but one of the other men had his hand painfully over her mouth.

Later, she remembered that they tied her to a donkey. She drifted in and out of consciousness, barely aware of her surroundings. All she remembered was that Ramón walked beside her every step of the way. He no longer seemed cowed in her presence, no longer seemed apologetic. He stood straight, staring into the distance. Proud.

When they brought her to the well, he was the one who mounted her onto his shoulder. He was the one who paused before dropping her in.

He looked into her eyes and said: "I don't hear anyone laughing at me now, Señorita Hacienda."

The fall knocked her unconscious, and she remembered no more.

* * *

Delfina's heart sank like a stone. She knew where the posse inside her was headed next: the little *kiosco* where she'd purchased the water the day before. The young man who'd told her he couldn't go to Buenos Aires because of the voices in his head wasn't simply descended from the Ramón of the memories… he was the very same man, complete with the muscles Señorita Hacienda had admired in spite of herself.

She walked down the center of the empty street, reveling in the feeling that she owned the town. Delfina suspected that the feeling might belong to one of the multitude within her… but she knew it also might be her own. She'd often felt powerless, living in a society that, at times, seemed to be completely devoid of justice. The insanity she was living in now, at least had the redeeming characteristic that justice was being served. Direct, perhaps uncivilized, but fair and satisfying.

The kiosco was empty, and the light was out, even though the window was open to the night. Had there been anyone else alive on the streets of the town, they could have helped themselves to a free smorgasbord of chocolate and candy.

But, of course, no one walked the streets of this town save the vengeful spirits of the wrongfully dead.

She climbed through the window, struggling against the resistance offered by the passage from exterior to interior, and scattering boxes of gum and cigarettes all over the floor. She knew he was inside. His voices would have warned him that she was coming… but he would never have dared to go outside, not at night. He'd be hiding inside the house adjacent to the kiosco, hoping the roof over his head would keep him as safe as it always had.

"This is as far as I want to go," she said. "You're inside. Whoever wants to go get him can go right ahead. I don't want to watch."

She braced for another bout in the well as her punishment for rebelling against the will of the ghosts inside her, but all that happened was that a single wisp of smoke emerged from her and coalesced into a dark monster.

This one had a humanoid form—two legs, two arms, a head—but was covered in scales that glistened in the light from the street. It oozed a sense of power, and it looked strong enough to tear down the masonry of the house around them using nothing but its clawed fingers.

None of that was the most terrifying thing about this monster, however. That aspect was the enormous erect phallus it sported, a barbed excrescence that appeared to have been designed to inflict the maximum amount of pain to anyone on the receiving end.

Ignoring Delfina, the monster began to chuckle to itself as it searched the little room behind the kiosco. The chuckling grew louder as it disappeared into the next room.

Delfina tracked its movements, laugh by laugh, through the darkened interior of the house. Then she tried to figure out who might have occupied that form. It seemed more like the kind of shape a man would use to punish a woman who'd wronged him. She wouldn't have been surprised to see the colonel using it on María. But it was Señorita Hacienda's memories that were missing from the collective zoo in her head.

Delfina grimaced.

She tried not to listen as the laughter suddenly turned gleeful, and a man's shout of terror broke through. The sounds soon dissolved into the noise of struggle, followed by groans of pain that grew ever louder and more anguished, accompanied by laughter that joined the crescendo.

The volume of it was so loud that, even covering her ears—which seemed to annoy the other spirits within—couldn't drown out what was happening.

In the end, she succumbed and listened as the Hacienda girl lived out the fantasy that must have obsessed her for centuries. Her revenge didn't come with the pain. It didn't come with her tormentor's death or even, she thought with the man's physical violation. Her utter and final revenge was expressed in the laughter, repetitive, endless, unforgettable laughter that would be the very last thing Ramón heard.

No matter what else he thought about what was happening to him as his insides were torn to shreds by that horrific organ, the laughter was the message he would take with him into the darkness.

Delfina was shellshocked by the violence, to the point where she missed when it ended. At some point, the laughter subsided back into a chuckle, and the monster returned into the room with Delfina, chortling quietly and glistening with gore. Then, as Delfina waited to see what it would do next, it simply melted back into smoke, which reentered Delfina.

As quickly as she'd lost them, she had Señorita Hacienda's memories back. With some new ones that Delfina didn't wish to explore.

* * *

They visited three more houses. At each door, Delfina wondered what kind of monster she was. Now that she knew exactly what would happen when she carried her unholy cargo across the threshold, she could no longer claim innocence. By aiding the dead citizens of Carrizo, she was murdering the living.

Nevertheless, after a second's hesitation, Delfina opened each door, pushed through each resisting threshold and released the demons into the interior of the homes of people she'd never seen, and who, most likely, had no inkling of what was coming for them.

It was that or face the well. She had no illusions about what awaited her if she didn't cooperate: eternity under the weight of dead bodies in the well... forever trapped right at the painful verge of suffocation. She would do anything to avoid that.

In each case, however, she refused to watch the dismemberment of the victim—or in the case of the second house, the family of victims. She crossed into the house, released her cargo, and waited for the screaming to stop.

Sometimes, the monsters she released would be content with whatever revenge obsessed them. Others, like the Hacienda girl, clearly wanted to personally witness the punishment of everyone who'd harmed them and their families. Those shades returned to Delfina once their own work was done. In one case—in the third of the houses—none of the spirits emerged immediately and Delfina felt some confusion within before a couple of black creatures materialized and quickly dispatched whoever lived in the house before returning. Apparently this was someone who hadn't been guilty of much more than supporting the wrong side, and no one had any particular hatred for whoever it was.

A pressure had been building inside Delfina, but was still undefined. The townsfolk inside her appeared to be of two different minds about… something. One half seemed to want to keep doing what they were doing, while the other—and she could somehow feel the colonel's wife among those—appeared to want to go to one very specific spot. The pressure was the instruction of where that spot lay.

Finally, the resistance subsided, and the single destination became clear in Delfina's mind. A house outside the town, on a narrow—but paved—road halfway up the hill. She would go there, next.

As she reached the end of the built-up portion of the main road, she looked up the hill and spotted the house. It was easy to see, since the streetlights illuminated the little road and showed that it held only one dwelling.

Even if it had been completely dark outside, the house would have been visible: a single yellow light shone in a window on the upper floor—the house was unlike any other house in the town in that it was built on two stories, and also in that it had a chalet-like design, with a slanted roof, as if it had been imported from Switzerland and dropped in the hot, arid, and snowless territory it now graced.

Delfina trudged up the street and found herself wishing the townspeople's magic extended beyond terrorizing villagers and making time run like tapioca pudding—the night should have been over ages ago—to practical considerations like flying from one place to another so Delfina didn't have to walk.

A block away from the house, she stopped. "There's

someone standing outside. On the street I think it's a woman."

A flurry of consternation flashed through the host inside her, but it only lasted for a moment before the consensus, driven by the overpowering personality of the colonel's wife came through to her: keep going.

Delfina shrugged and walked on. It was all the same to her. Kill people inside or outside. Whatever.

She stopped about five meters away. The figure was, in fact, a woman. She wore the classic poncho of the region's indigenous population, and had her hair tied back in a loose ponytail.

The face was that of Tierca, the woman who'd cursed the townsfolk.

On that day in front of the well, the witch-woman had appeared calm, vindictive, certain of her decision. Now her eyes were haunted, and Delfina could see every moment of the past two hundred years etched into her face. Every second in which the realization that she'd made a terrible, awful mistake weighed on her soul.

Insanity lurked in those eyes. But something else as well: a mad, desperate hope.

Tierca said something in a guttural tongue. Then she fixed her eyes on Delfina and said, in rough Spanish: "I'm glad you came. I've been carrying this magic for what seems like eternity. Passing it to you is a pleasure."

She spat on the ground, and the world twirled about. The spirits within her raged…

And then went silent.

* * *

There was no well, no dark cave, and no misty field. In fact the space she occupied appeared to be notable mainly for the lack of long-dead Spaniards asking her to abandon the life and attitudes of the twenty-first century to take part in their bloody vendettas.

The place was a mountain. A tall one. The sun shone on her from a perfectly clear blue sky while Delfina looked down on pillow-like clouds below.

Stone, chipped and ground to gravel by glaciers in places and hard and vertical in others, surrounded her. She shivered as the crisp air caressed her unprotected skin.

On looking around, she sensed that something was off. The sky, the clouds, the other mountains in the distance didn't seem to be correctly positioned in relation to each other, as if the whole thing had been drawn by that guy who did the mind-bending buildings where the stairs went up to arrive at the bottom. She tried to remember his name. Esper. Esther. Something like that.

As she attempted to focus, the entire panorama changed perspective and contracted around her to the point in which she could reach out and touch everything in sight.

Delfina yelped, thinking the landscape was going to crush her. She held out her hand, the terror of yet another experience of being suffocated by irresistible forces overcoming her fear of the approaching scenery.

She wasn't crushed, however. Like those optical illusions, the approach of the distant objects happened mostly inside her mind. The mountains were both right beside her and off in the middle distance. She was present both in an infinite landscape and locked inside a tiny room with the entire world.

After a few moments that stretched like an eternity, Delfina took a tentative step. Her feet went down a path that stretched forever.

And her head bumped into a rocky outcrop that she would have sworn was a mile off.

She rubbed her head and cursed. Then, feeling her way, she sat on a patch of cold mountain grass, short and dry, to look around again.

I should be terrified, she thought. She wasn't, though. A man following her on a dark street in the city would terrify her. Being stalked by a lion on the African plains would immobilize her with fear. But just a wonky landscape? She saw more terrifying things on her iPad in the morning.

Is that really it? You watched a woman get torn to pieces just a while ago. Was that also something you see every day? The voice of her reason asked.

Delfina didn't know what to say to that. She tried to remember what she'd felt watching the monsters butcher María. She'd felt… nothing. Like it was a film, carefully stage-managed for her enjoyment. She'd watched in the way she'd watch a slasher flick with her girlfriends, the sick thrill overcoming the raw viscerality of the experience. Watching with the intellect while shutting of any feeling.

Now, stuck in a maze of broken dimensions, perhaps forever, she felt the apathy of one who didn't believe that it actually applied to her. *Hell*, she thought, even if it does, *I'll just be stuck here forever. I won't die, won't feel any pain. Just eternal boredom.*

You'll go nuts.

"I'm already going nuts," she replied. "I'm talking to myself."

Her words made the reality around her shake and vibrate.

Delfina stood to explore and immediately realized she wasn't alone. She turned back to see a man wearing a hockey mask, behind her. In one hand, he carried a bloody machete. In the other, he held the severed head of a woman by the hair. The head bounced up and down as he stalked her.

She ran forward, the man ran after her.

It was exactly the situation she'd imagined while thinking of the slasher film.

The man stopped and tore off his mask to reveal Joaco's face underneath. Joaco discarded the mask and looked down at the head he carried. He threw that away, too, and grinned at Delfina.

"So you don't like my poetry," he said.

"I never said that," she replied.

"You did. But that doesn't matter. You didn't need to. I saw it in your face. You never really respected me. I was just a game to you, a toy to help you get back at your family. A rebellion against your own upbringing and people."

"That's stupid," she said. "I liked you well enough."

"You're lying. To me, or to yourself. But you're lying."

She squared up to face him. "And you're not even real. You're just a figment of this place, put here to scare me."

Joaco smiled an ugly smile. He brought the blade up and, even though he seemed to be standing ten steps away, it appeared right beneath her nose. Delfina smelled the coppery tang of blood. "I don't need you to believe in me for it to hurt. I'm going to get my revenge."

"Your revenge? Are you serious? You were the one who…"

Delfina screamed as the machete flicked up and sliced into the bare flesh of her arm.

Aloofness vanished. Intellect folded. Delfina turned and ran, no more sentient than a gazelle impelled by instinct to try to escape a cheetah. She ran until she bounced off a rock, ran again until her head froze because the top of the sky was closer than it looked. Then she stopped because her flight pierced the clouds and she couldn't see where she was going.

Joaco's footsteps, however, echoed as if he was following her through a tunnel. Actually, it sounded as if he was ahead of her.

She turned, panting, out of breath, with her chest tight from terror, searching for him. His footfalls came from ahead. Now from the right. She felt an itch between her shoulder blades, as if that was the place where he would bury the machete and end her existence.

"You're not really here!" she said. "You're just a monster put there by my imagination. I was thinking about slasher films."

"And you were thinking about me, too?" His voice seemed to come from above.

She thought about it. Had she been thinking about him? Consciously? Unconsciously? No.

"I couldn't care less about you."

"I know," he said. "I've known it since the first time I fucked you. You didn't care about me. Hell, you didn't even enjoy it all that much." He paused. "I thought, maybe, if I took you on vacation, you'd understand me a bit better. And you'd respect me. I was wrong."

"You don't really exist."

"Tell yourself that if you want," Joaco replied. "It won't make any difference."

Instinct—the same that told the gazelle that a big cat hid in the grass, even though the gazelle couldn't see it—told Delfina to duck. As she did so, the blade whistled through the air above her.

She ran again.

"You can't get out," the voice behind her said. "You can only run forever. And even if you run forever, I'll catch you."

Her vision cleared, and Delfina realized she was under the clouds now. Still high on a mountain, but not as high as before. Below her stretched the little town of Carrizo, but not like she knew it. It floated in an island of sky, surrounded on all sides like something in a video game where you needed to level up to get a glider or something to reach it.

This wasn't a video game. She wasn't leveling up.

"I can see you now," Joaco said. "Just give up. Why suffer more than you need to?"

He took a step and appeared beside her. She jumped back to get some distance.

The town was right there. If only she could reach it, she'd have her army of dead Spaniards again. Joaco would be the one running if that happened… she'd ask the colonel's wife to run him down but not kill him. Just hamstring him and make him crawl.

What are you even talking about? This isn't really Joaco. He might have been a dick, but he isn't a murderer.

The voice in her head was right. Completely correct. Joaco's presence was the result of the way Carrizo worked: everything you believed was real. If you believed in Christianity, you could live forever in God's light. But only if you avoided getting cursed by someone who believed in… whatever it was the old witch believed in. And if you happened to think of an ancient eighties horror movie, the protagonist would come to make your eternal curse even less pleasant than otherwise. It seemed that any belief anyone had ever held would function.

Except her own belief in God. That didn't seem to have protected her in the least.

She stopped dead in her tracks and Joaco overstepped and missed her. Had she really expressed any belief in a Deity? When was the last time she thought about God? She must have been a little girl.

She still believed… but she'd been so disenchanted with the church that she had suppressed all of her feelings, just believing… nothing.

Delfina knew she'd never believe in the full Catholic Trinity. But that wasn't what was needed. If her belief in serial killers wearing hockey masks could be used against her… then her much deeper-seated belief in God had to help.

Joaco charged her. His free hand managed to get a grip on her shirt, and she had to twist out of his grip. She fell to her knees and, again, Joaco overshot and stumbled into the distance.

As she knelt on the loose stones her left hand went to the neck of her t-shirt, and she pulled on the thin gold chain she'd worn since she was a small girl. From the tiny links hung a gold cross, a gift from her grandmother, which had belonged to some great aunt or other. Her other hand struggled to find a rock to throw at Joaco, but she ended up with a jagged thing too big to get any distance with.

Joaco had turned back. He saw her brandishing the little cross and laughed. "You think you're going to stop me with that? Your little god has no power here, and you always acted like you don't believe in him anyway." He laughed. "But then again, it's always been the tradition of your class to run roughshod over everyone and do everything your own religion considers wrong only to repent on your deathbed, make a quick confession and have everything forgiven. Unfortunately, it doesn't work this way."

"I never stopped believing," she whispered.

"What? I can't hear you," he replied, tone mocking.

Delfina spoke louder. "I said I never stopped believing." She took a step towards him, which seemed to amuse rather than surprise Joaco. But the geometry of the crumpled mountains played tricks on her, and her first step deposited her slightly off to his right.

"You know that isn't true." He smirked at her. "Your priests and your parents would have been quite shocked to see some of the things you did with me. Aren't you supposed to be a virgin until you get married?"

"Churches say a lot of things," she said, taking another step towards him. "But God never spoke to me directly." To her surprise, she appeared right next to him, perfectly placed for him to run her through with his machete.

But Joaco was just as surprised to suddenly find her there as she was, especially when she leaned over far enough to place the cross on his head and say· "Feel the power of the God I believe in."

He pulled his head away and laughed. "And that is how it ends for you."

Joaco thrust with his machete. Delfina jerked away, but not quite fast enough. She felt the blade slice through the skin of her side, bouncing off ribs and leaving a line of fire as it went. For a moment, she was caught in his embrace, close enough that she could smell him.

She braced herself for the funk of the grave, the smell of overripe zombie or of nothing at all, the odor of dream stuff. But Joaco smelled exactly the way he always did. Slightly of floral deodorant, slightly of sweat. Even the faintest scent of the fabric softener he insisted on for some reason.

The pain in her side reminded her that, smelling genuine or not, he was trying to kill her. Delfina pulled herself away, then brought her right hand down as he overbalanced and stumbled. The jagged rock went into the skull of the apparition that wore Joaco's face and body, and he fell face-down onto the rocks. He shuddered once, then lay still.

The maze of crumpled reality around her didn't dissolve into nothingness the way she'd been expecting it to. Delfina still found herself trapped in the three-dimensional mind-bender.

She looked down at Joaco's corpse, accusingly, to see that it seemed to be blurring at the edges where she'd rammed the rock through his skull. She knelt and pushed her hand into the weird illusion.

Her hand sank through the skin and also through the reality around the dead Joaco.

She pulled it back.

Where her hand had entered, a dark hole remained. When she looked through, she couldn't see what was on the other side. Just nothingness, it seemed.

Delfina studied her hand. It was unhurt. Passing into the void beyond this reality had done her no harm.

"Screw it." She put both hands into the blackness and pulled at the edges. Reality itself ripped at the seams, opening a patch of blackness first as long as her arm, then as her leg, finally longer than she was.

By now, the tear was opening on its own, without her help, like a boulder rolling downhill. Threads of reality almost too small to see unwound around the frayed edges. Within moments, the tear was extending into the distance. A tendril of blackness stretched beneath her feet and the ground under her disappeared.

Delfina fell through.

And found herself back on the rising mountain street, face to face with the Tierca, who appeared to have tied her up and was stacking wood around her feet. A gas can and a box of matches sat on the pavement beside Delfina, and she felt the spirits in her hear screaming, their desire obvious: they were desperate to get out.

Delfina simply separated her arms from her body, and the clothesline she'd been tied with popped apart, no match for the strength of an entire village. Then she kicked the wood away.

Tierca looked up, the hope completely gone, replaced by fear. She said something in the unknown language she'd used before, but her scream, her hoarseness, told Delfina the curse wouldn't be as potent as the one before.

As soon as she woke, the wisps began to emerge. No less than ten monsters appeared. Eight bent and misshapen forms began to crawl, slither and slink towards the witch, who backed away with her hands in front of her.

Two tall, straight monsters, featureless except for a certain roundness of the hips in one denoting a female form, and a certain accentuation of the shoulders denoting a male companion walked behind the attackers, goading them on. Of all the monsters, only these appeared to have any sort of dignity, like vampires in among half-changed lycanthropes. They ruled over the dead, monarchs of the night.

Delfina immediately identified Tomás and the colonel's wife.

The monsters nipped at the retreating witch like jackals keeping a buffalo at bay. Though the witch wasn't a large woman, anyone could see she was the most powerful of the presences in that patch of road. She would spit and curse, and the nearest monster would recoil, hissing, with each assault.

But there were too many of the monsters. Her curses could only hurt them, not incapacitate them, and before long, a catlike, slinking thing managed to rake her leg with its claws. It did so at the cost of getting cursed at point-blank range… but it did so.

Tierca stumbled and limped back. Another creature, a crocodilian on all fours, sank its teeth into an ankle, which cracked in the night. Again, a curse dislodged it, but the witch now dragged a leg along the ground.

She tried to head for the house, but the circle closed behind her, and monsters began to come closer and closer.

The cat-thing managed to claw her in the hamstring, and Tierca toppled over backward. One of the monsters began to gnaw on an outstretched hand. Delfina looked away as it tore off a finger.

The woman-monster lifted an arm, and the monsters halted their attack. The two elegant forms walked to the prone witch and looked over her. Tierca glared back.

Delfina realized they must be communicating on some plane she didn't have access to. It wasn't hard to deduce that one side was gloating, the other was telling them to rot in hell, and it was over in moments. The woman-form made a careless gesture and the misshapen monsters began again.

Tierca didn't die quickly, but she died thoroughly. The monsters tore through her extremities like they were being paid to keep her alive as long as possible. Blood soaked into the pavement, then saturated the area and began to flow downhill.

As the old witch was slowly devoured, she kept her dark, hate-filled eyes squarely on the two taller figures until the eyes were torn out by a snake-like thing with tiny hands.

Finally, the witch's head slumped forward in death.

She hadn't screamed or made any sound denoting pain. Not even once.

* * *

Except for a couple that wandered off into the night, apparently satisfied with killing their tormentor, most of the undead posse returned to Delfina. They grimly got back to work, entering houses and butchering their occupants.

Still, Delfina knew there was more to be done, for a simple reason: there had been no sign of Güiraldes. Now that the witch was dead, and the battle was won, apparently they were murdering his people in order to reach him last.

Delfina suspected his murder would make the lingering deaths she'd already seen look like a mother's caress.

She allowed herself to be prodded this way and that, mindlessly following the dictates of the mob within, and doing her best to ignore the carnage she witnessed as they breached each house. Her arm bled from the machete wound, and she staunched it with a strip cut from her shirt with a scissors she'd found in a family house while the inhabitants were being slaughtered. Her clothes were completely ruined.

The night dragged on, and she just put one foot in front of the other until she suddenly found herself jerked back into full consciousness by a sudden familiarity.

Delfina faced the door into Doña Julia's compound.

She hesitated. The old woman had been open, welcoming, accepting. Could Delfina really bring death onto her head?

She gritted her teeth. If it meant avoiding the well, she'd kill her own mother.

Delfina walked into the garden, then opened the front door and entered.

Wisps of smoke flew in every direction. More than at any spot before. More than she thought still remained. By the time the monsters stood before her, she felt weak—almost all of her extra strength had gone. So few memories of life in the early nineteenth century remained. Delfina had to lean on a door to catch her breath. Pain radiated from her arm.

The monsters dispersed, splintering doors and howling. Doña Julia appeared, only to be buried under a mass of black forms.

Every room, it seemed, had been occupied by someone the monsters wanted to kill. The sobbing woman from the room next to hers went silent.

The only two black figures not participating in the orgy of death were the colonel's wife and Tomás. They walked through the carnage like a pair of generals inspecting the previous day's battlefield.

Grimly, Delfina followed.

The hallway went almost all the way around the building, ending at an ornate wooden door.

The door opened to reveal a large bedroom in the colonial style. Güiraldes was nowhere to be seen.

Tomás pushed the bed aside to reveal a trembling form underneath. The black figure laughed, the only sound she'd heard one of those two make, and pulled the man out with one hand around his chest.

"No. Please, no. I'm sorry. I'm sorry!"

Tomas put a gentle finger of its free hand on Güiraldes' lips.

The little man shut up.

Then the black figure clamped the rest of that hand down over Güiraldes' mouth and, holding the man's torso with its other hand, pulled the former revolutionary's head all the way around with an audible snap.

Tomás dropped the corpse—looking back over its shoulder now—onto the floor and bowed to Delfina.

Then he offered the colonel's wife its hand and they

walked into the night, leaving Delfina alone in a house full of corpses.

Not knowing what to do, and dizzy from exhaustion, she dragged herself back to her own room, glanced at the silhouette in the window—still seated at the desk—and dropped onto the bed.

She was out before her head landed on the linen.

* * *

It was the same field, the same mist, the same feeling of old death.

Delfina stood alone in the swaying grass, awaiting judgment. A small bubble in the mist, a slightly larger cloud, emerged and expanded. Finally, it filled out to take the form of a man.

He wore a helmet and mail, over which a white tunic with a red cross pattern hung, too big for the skeletal inhabitant of the chain shirt.

The specter approached with long strides and stood before her, as if waiting. Delfina didn't know what was expected of her. Was she supposed to kneel? To bow? To run for her life?

She had no clue, so she did nothing.

The apparition waited another pair of beats, then shrugged and raised a sword it held—had that been there before?—to Delfina's shoulder.

The knight lowered the blade, nodded once, and walked back into the mist, dissolving as he went.

As soon as he disappeared, sun peeked out from between the clouds and burned the mist away, to leave her standing in a gentle emerald sea.

* * *

Delfina blinked. The sun through the window seemed to be focused precisely on her head. Joaco was seated in his habitual spot beside the window.

"I had the strangest dream," she said, jumping out of bed.

She felt wonderful, more awake and alert than she had in ages. Nothing could stop her now... and if Joaco insisted on pretending to write his poetry, she would simply shake him until he stopped the nonsense.

Two steps took her over to where he was seated, and she put her hand on his shoulder.

He collapsed onto the desk.

The back of his head had been caved in. It looked like the wound a sharpened rock would make.

She stifled her scream and walked into the hall. Flies buzzed around dismembered, half-eaten corpses.

Delfina ran outside and retched, not wanting to ruin the carpet which, she realized as she tried to vomit, was stupid: the gore would never come out.

After a frustrating series of heaves, she gave up: when was the last time she'd eaten? Certainly before the endless night of murder and mayhem.

The thought of food made her want to vomit again, and the heaves lasted longer this time.

Finally, she walked out of the compound.

Carrizo felt even more desolate than usual. The streets were still empty, but now the sensation wasn't of people safe inside their houses away from the mountain sun, but of... nothing.

Delfina walked to Joaco's car. She could get the keys from the room, drive away forever. But no. Someone would find his body. Someone would realize it had been murdered with a rock, not attacked by whatever had torn the rest of the town to pieces. Someone would blame the woman who'd stolen his car.

She walked down the road towards the traffic circle, careful to stay as far from the place where a pack of dogs were feeding on the meat that lay discarded there.

As she crossed the bridge over the stream, the town shimmered behind her, in a haze that made it difficult to see.

Delfina looked both ways along the highway. There didn't seem to be anyone coming, and the heat was suffocating.

She didn't feel that she could walk all the way to Salta anymore.

But she felt good. She could probably make it to the next town at least. Probably even jog there.

* * *

* * *

The judge took the stand and looked around the courtroom. On Delfina's side, only her parents had come to hear the verdict. Her lawyer looked confident, but Delfina's heart fluttered in her chest. The process, the gathering of testimony and the police investigations had been the worst six months of her life.

On the other side of the courtroom, about twenty people sat, talking loudly and holding up a banner that read: *Justice for Joaquín.* They were members of a political group that had attempted to make a *cause celebre* out of Joaco's disappearance, to paint Delfina as the well-connected rich girl who'd murdered her working-class boyfriend and made the body disappear.

Every once in a while, one of them would take a moment to glare at the defense.

Delfina sat quietly as the judge organized his papers. The trial hadn't been what she'd expected. Argentina didn't have a jury system or even public hearings, like she saw on TV. Evidence and arguments were presented to the judge through a series of written documents, and hearings were only held for the formal arraignment and, today, for the delivery of the verdict.

To her relief, there were no reporters present. Her lawyer had warned her the activists might have been able to bully a few, but that more likely, the press had better things to do than harass an innocent young woman. That had certainly proved to be the case so far, at least: only the left-leaning *Página 12* had even bothered to say anything about the case, and that was just to wonder whether it hadn't been Delfina at all, but the Salta Police that had been responsible for the mysterious disappearance of a young man and his car. No one had paid that article any notice, and none of the serious media companies had covered the trial.

The judge was a woman in her late sixties, a peroxide blonde with rectangular glasses and a severe expression. She read the formalities of the verdict, the date, the names of the plaintiff—the Argentine Federal Government—and the defendant—Delfina—and the name of the court.

Then, after reading the accusations, she said: "In light of the complete lack of any but the most circumstantial evidence, in which a citizen was accused of murder without the existence of a body, of witnesses or, indeed of any physical evidence, the verdict of this court is that the defendant is innocent of all charges."

The members of the political party, who'd been speaking amongst themselves went completely silent.

The judge continued. "In fact, my decision has the specific opinion that this case was a waste of the court's time and taxpayer money, based on the evidence presented, and I have entered the technical reasons for that in the verdict. If a superior court is asked to review this process, I have recommended that they take the technical deficiencies into consideration when reviewing if an appeal is acceptable."

One of the young men on the defense's side of the small audience room stood. "You're a tool of the dictatorship!" he shouted. "You want the country to belong to the same corporate powers that have been running it since it was founded. You're a disgrace to the constitution." He turned to his friends, who were sitting silently. Getting no support, he continued. "I would call you a disgrace to the Judicial Branch, but that, sadly, is impossible. If you were honest, you'd send this murderer to prison forever, and her parents, too. There's no way she could have done this alone. There were powerful co-conspirators. This goes all the way to the top!"

The judge just smiled and said nothing. She stood but, before leaving the courtroom, the spoke to the captain of the security forces present: "Please make sure that none of the people in this room try to use violence against the innocent citizen who has been subjected to a mockery of the penal system."

The man nodded, the glint in his eyes clearly showing that he hoped the protesters would try something. Then he got to work clearing the courtroom of all bystanders not directly involved with the trial. Soon, Delfina, her parents, her lawyer and the prosecutor stood alone in the room.

The prosecutor came over to Delfina and said: "Congratulations. There's no way the state can appeal with that verdict and opinion in the books. Whoever tried would lose their job." He shook her lawyer's hand. "I'm glad you got off, and I hope I never get assigned to another case like this one. I know it's all political, and that the defendant being from an important family meant it would have looked bad if there had been no investigation, but everyone knows this was a mistake."

"Politics," Delfina's lawyer said with a shrug. The prosecutor left.

Delfina sat there, feeling empty. That was it? There would be no further consequences for killing Joaco and abandoning his corpse in a ghost town that disappeared after she walked away?

It felt wrong. If she'd gotten a verdict of self-defense, at least she would have felt that that night in the province of Salta meant something. But this? It was like nothing had ever happened.

Her mother tugged on her hand and gripped her in a huge embrace, then she broke down, crying like a baby.

"It's all right, mom. Didn't you hear? I'm innocent."

"But what they did to you... all of this..."

Delfina patted her head. "I'm fine. Really. Everyone's been telling me it was going to be all right all this time. I believed you. I wasn't worried."

Her mother's face said that she didn't believe that, that she'd been worried because Delfina had been quiet and withdrawn since she'd come back from that awful trip with that awful man. She hoped her mother wouldn't start all over again. She really wasn't in the mood for it.

In fact, the verdict had made her angry.

Angry at Joaco for blowing her off in the most bizarre way possible. Angry about what had happened to her in that town which months of googling told her had ceased to exist more than two hundred years earlier. And most of all, angry about the fact that she felt nothing—no guilt, no sadness, no revulsion, no remorse—about any of the things that had happened on that fateful night. It was as if her capacity to feel anything, except the anger, had been taken away.

She stood and followed her entourage out the door, with a policeman at the head and tail of the procession, to make sure no one tried to assault them. The group had only been verbally abusive thus far, but with their hopes so thoroughly thwarted, everyone was on edge wondering what they might try next.

It turned out they tried nothing, and Delfina reached her car unmolested, and was driven out of the city proper to her house in San Isidro.

At her mother's insistence, she rested.

Until her phone rang. It was Luciana, her best friend, the girl who'd pretty much been her partner-in-crime since she was in pre-school for two-year-olds.

"I heard," Luciana said, her voice almost too excited to be contained by the phone lines. "Woohoo. I knew they wouldn't lock you up. Anyone who thinks you could kill someone—even someone like Joaco—just doesn't know you. We need to celebrate. I'll pick you up at eight."

"No, I…"

"Don't even think about it," Luciana said. "I put up with you avoiding me because of the trial. And yes, I get it. You must be fucking exhausted. But you're going to sleep tomorrow. Tonight, we're going to celebrate. My treat. I will see you at eight." She hung up.

Delfina dressed unenthusiastically. At about seven, she nearly called to cancel, but she imagined Luciana's response and hung up.

Luciana arrived exactly on time and they drove to a restaurant in the city center. She spoke the entire drive, enthusiastically telling Delfina just what a great person she was.

It was almost impossible to remain gloomy in presence of such unrelenting joy. Especially when the joy was being expressed on Delfina's behalf. For a while, she chatted and laughed, and they drank a bottle of wine between them. The food was excellent.

"Give me a minute," Delfina said. "I need to go to the bathroom."

As she picked her way back through the crowded restaurant, Delfina suddenly felt the sense that something wanted her to go somewhere.

Oh, no.

Instead of heading back towards the table, she took a different path and burst out of the restaurant.

"Should I get your car?" the valet said.

"No, no," she said, as she hurried away.

The restaurant was in the city center, surrounded by office blocks that loomed, empty over the city. The sidewalk was full of uncollected trash bags.

Just around the corner from the restaurants, footsteps echoed, and Delfina looked behind. A man walked, head down, hands in his pockets, on the sidewalk directly to her rear.

Delfina shrugged and kept going.

The man's footsteps drew nearer. She crossed the

empty street. The man remained on the same sidewalk, now moving parallel to her.

She glanced over just as the man walked under a streetlight. He was in his late twenties, with dark longish hair and, for a fleeting moment, she thought it was Joaco, back from whatever limbo she'd confined him to. But the moment passed, and she realized that the man wasn't Joaco… but he was still familiar.

She stopped and peered at him. By now, the man had noticed her scrutiny and stood facing her.

Finally, Delfina realized where she'd seen him before, and gasped: it was one of the men from the audience at court. One of the protesters. The only one who'd spoken out against the verdict.

"You," she said, accusingly. "Why are you following me?"

"You know why," he said in a voice loud enough to carry across the street. "You killed that poor man. And your family covered up for you. And then the law said you were innocent. Because that's the way justice works here in Argentina: the rich never pay for their crimes."

"I'm not rich," she said. "My family might be well-to-do, but it's not like we drive Ferraris or…"

"Compared to that poor boy you murdered, you're from a different world," the man replied.

"I didn't murder him! It was self-defense. He wanted to kill me!"

The other straightened, mouth agape. "So you admit it. You killed him. And then you covered it up. We were right… and there's no way the police and the judge could have been fooled." He slapped his hand against his leg. "They knew. They knew and they covered for you."

"That's stupid. No one knew anything," Delfina replied. "I was alone. And Joaco tried to kill me."

"Do you think I'm stupid?" The man's face was red with fury. He took a few tentative steps toward Delfina. "I'm not. You killed him. But I'm also not stupid enough to think I can change anything. I didn't come here to get a confession. You can confess all day, and no one would believe me."

He put his hand in his pocket and a streetlight reflected against something. At first, Delfina thought it was just a cell phone, that he would try to coerce her into admitting she'd killed Joaco. But there was something about that reflection…

A knife.

The guy held it up in the light so that Delfina could see it clearly. He took another step. Then he rushed her.

Delfina barely managed to avoid the first wild swing. The man turned to face her again, an ugly grin on his face. "You're going to die. Bleed out in an alley. A life for a life."

Delfina finally felt something again: terror. Like with Joaco, it was her life that was endangered now, not the lives of some townsfolk she'd never met. She trembled. "Don't…"

The man's grin widened. "Did he beg for you to spare him? Did you laugh?"

He chuckled. Delfina took a step back.

Suddenly, three wisps of smoke began to seep from her. She looked at them dumbly, and the man followed her gaze.

"Are you on fire?" he said.

Delfina returned his grin. "No. But I have a feeling I'm going to enjoy what happens next," she replied.

Three black monsters coalesced from the smoke. One was a kind of hairy spiked ball. Another was a tentacled snake. The third was a misshapen man-form that advanced on all fours.

The snake form reached her assailant first. The man didn't even manage to put up his knife before it snapped his knee in half at the leg.

The other two surged forward and Delfina turned away.

"Goodbye," she called over her shoulder as the screams grew louder.

* * *

"I thought you weren't coming back," Luciana said when she sat at the table again."

"Sorry, I wasn't feeling great," Delfina replied.

Concern flashed over Luciana's features. "Oh. Dammit. I'm sorry. I shouldn't have insisted. I'm a disaster. I'll take you home."

"What?" Delfina said. "I'm feeling much better now. In fact, I feel better than I've ever felt. We need to celebrate."

Luciana raised her glass. "To your life as a free woman."

Delfina grinned and raised her own. "And to my future life, which I think is going to be very different from now on."

They drank to it, and Delfina felt the approval radiating from the three companions she now carried with her.

THE END

About the Author

Gustavo Bondoni is an Argentine writer with over two hundred stories published in fourteen countries, in seven languages. He is a winner in the National Space Society's "Return to Luna" Contest, the Marooned Award for Flash Fiction, 2016 SFReader Short Story Award, and 2018 N3F Fiction Award. His sort fiction has been published in *Swords and Sorcery, Albedo One, M-Brane*, and many anthologies.

He has written several novels in multiple genres, including science fiction *Outside* (from Guardbridge Books), *Siege* and *Incursion*; comic fantasy *The Malakiad*; and modern thriller *Timeless*. Surely, more are to come.

He now lives in Buenos Aires with his wife and children. Follow him online at:

http://gustavobondoni.com.